园丁集

The Gardener

［印］泰戈尔（Rabindranath Tagore）◎著

冰心◎译

湖南文艺出版社 HUNAN LITERATURE AND ART PUBLISHING HOUSE 博集天卷 CS-BOOKY

图书在版编目（CIP）数据

园丁集 /（印）泰戈尔（Rabindranath Tagore）著；
冰心译 . -- 长沙：湖南文艺出版社，2019.6
书名原文：The Gardener
ISBN 978-7-5404-9243-4

Ⅰ . ①园… Ⅱ . ①泰… ②冰… Ⅲ . ①诗集－印度－
现代 Ⅳ . ① I351.25

中国版本图书馆 CIP 数据核字（2019）第 095626 号

上架建议：名家经典·文学

YUANDING JI
园丁集

作　　者：[印]泰戈尔（Rabindranath Tagore）
译　　者：冰　心
出 版 人：曾赛丰
责任编辑：薛　健　刘诗哲
监　　制：蔡明菲　邢越超
特约策划：王　维
特约编辑：蔡文婷
版权支持：辛　艳
营销支持：傅婷婷　文刀刀　周　茜
装帧设计：潘雪琴
内文排版：百朗文化
出版发行：湖南文艺出版社
　　　　　（长沙市雨花区东二环一段 508 号　邮编：410014）
网　　址：www.hnwy.net
印　　刷：三河市兴博印务有限公司
经　　销：新华书店
开　　本：880mm×1230mm　1/32
字　　数：200 千字
印　　张：7
版　　次：2019 年 6 月第 1 版
印　　次：2019 年 6 月第 1 次印刷
书　　号：ISBN 978-7-5404-9243-4
定　　价：42.00 元

若有质量问题，请致电质量监督电话：010-59096394
团购电话：010-59320018

前言

　　许多批评家都说，诗人是"人类的儿童"。因为他们都是天真的，善良的。在现代的许多诗人中，泰戈尔（Rabindranath Tagore）更是一个"孩子天使"。他的诗正如这个天真烂漫的天使的脸；看着他，就"能够知道一切事物的意义"，就感得和平，感得安慰，并且知道真相爱。著"泰戈尔的哲学"的 S. Radhakrishnan 说：泰戈尔著作之流行，之能引起全世界人的兴趣，一半在于他思想中高超的理想主义，一半在于他作品中的文学的庄严与美丽。

　　泰戈尔是印度孟加拉（Bengal）地方的人。印度是一个"诗的国"。诗就是印度人日常生活的一部分，在这个"诗之国"里，产生了这个伟大的诗人泰戈尔自然是没有什么奇怪的。

　　泰戈尔的文学活动，开始得极早。他在十四岁的时候，即开始写剧本。他的著作，最初都是用孟加拉文写的；凡是说孟加拉文的地方，没有人不日日歌诵他的诗歌。后来他自己和他的朋友把许多作品陆续译成了英文，诗集有"园丁集"、"新月集"、"采果集"、"飞鸟集"、"吉檀迦利"、"爱者之礼物"与"歧道"；剧本有"牺牲及其他"、"邮局"、"暗室之王"、"春之循环"；论文集有"生之实现"、"人格"；杂著有"我的回忆"、"饿石及其他"、"家庭与世界"等。

在孟加拉文里，据印度人说：他的诗较英文写得更为美丽。

"他是我们圣人中的第一人：不拒绝生命，而能说出生命之本身的，这就是我们所以爱他的原因了。"

郑振铎

一九二二年六月二十六日

目录　|contents|

园丁集

The Gardener

仆人

请对您的仆人开恩吧，我的女王!

SERVANT

Have mercy upon your servant, my queen!

女王

集会已经开过，我的仆人们都走了。你为什么来得这么晚呢?

QUEEN

The assembly is over and my servants are all gone. Why do you come at this late hour?

仆人

您同别人谈过以后，就是我的时间了。

我来问有什么剩余的工作，好让您的最末一个仆人去做。

SERVANT

When you have finished with others, that is my time.

I come to ask what remains for your last servant to do.

女王

在这么晚的时间你还想做什么呢？

QUEEN

What can you expect when it is too late?

仆人

让我做您花园里的园丁吧。

SERVANT

Make me the gardener of your flower garden.

女王

这是什么傻想头呢?

QUEEN

What folly is this?

仆人

我要搁下别的工作。

我把我的剑矛扔在尘土里。不要差遣我去遥远的宫廷;不要命令我做新的征讨。只求您让我做花园里的园丁。

SERVANT

I will give up my other work.

I throw my swords and lances down in the dust. Do not send me to distant courts; do not bid me undertake new conquests. But make me the gardener of your flower garden.

女王

你的职责是什么呢?

QUEEN

What will your duties be?

仆人

为您闲散的日子服务。

我要保持你晨兴散步的草径清爽新鲜，您每一移步将有甘于就死的繁花以赞颂来欢迎您的双足。

我将在七叶树的枝间推送您的秋千；向晚的月亮将挣扎着从叶隙里吻您的衣裙。

我将在您床边的灯盏里添满香油，我将用檀香和番红花膏在您脚垫上涂画上美妙的花样。

SERVANT

The service of your idle days.

I will keep fresh the grassy path where you walk in the morning, where your feet will be greeted with praise at every step by the flowers eager for death.

I will swing you in a swing among the branches of the saptaparna, where the early evening moon will struggle to kiss your skirt through the leaves.

I will replenish with scented oil the lamp that burns by your bedside, and decorate your footstool with sandal and saffron paste in wondrous designs.

女王

你要什么酬报呢?

QUEEN

What will you have for your reward?

仆人

只要您允许我像握着嫩柔的菡萏一般地握住您的小拳,把花串套上您的纤腕;允许我用无忧花的红汁来染您的脚底,以亲吻来拂去那偶然留在那里的尘埃。

SERVANT

To be allowed to hold your little fists like tender lotusbuds and slip flower-chains over your wrists; to tinge the soles of your feet with the red juice of ashoka petals and kiss away the speck of dust that may chance to linger there.

女王

你的祈求被接受了，我的仆人，你将是我花园里的园丁。

QUEEN

Your prayers are granted, my servant, you will be the gardener of my flower garden.

002

"呵，诗人，夜晚渐临；你的头发已经变白。

"在你孤寂的沉思中听到了来生的消息么？"

"Ah, poet, the evening draws near; your hair is turning grey.

"Do you in your lonely musing hear the message of the hereafter?"

"是夜晚了，"诗人说，"夜虽已晚，我还在静听，因为也许有人会从村中呼唤。

"我看守着，是否有年轻的飘游的心聚在一起，两对渴望的眼睛切盼有音乐来打破他们的沉默，并替他们说话。

"如果我坐在生命的岸边默想着死亡和来世，又有谁来编写他们的热情的诗歌呢？

"It is evening," the poet said, "and I am listening because

some one may call from the village, late though it be.

"I watch if young straying hearts meet together and two pairs of eager eyes beg for music to break their silence and speak for them.

"Who is there to weave their passionate songs, if I sit on the shore of life and contemplate death and the beyond?

"早现的晚星消隐了。

"火葬灰中的红光在沉静的河边慢慢地熄灭下去。

"残月的微光下，胡狼从空宅的庭院里齐声嗥叫。

"假如有游子们离了家，到这里来守夜，低头静听黑暗的微语，有谁把生命的秘密向他耳边低诉呢，如果我关起门户，企图摆脱世俗的牵缠？

"The early evening star disappears.

"The glow of a funeral pyre slowly dies by the slient river.

"Jackals cry in chorus from the courtyard of the deserted house in the light of the worn-out moon.

"If some wanderer leaving home, come here to watch the night and with bowed head listen to the murmur of the darkness, who is there to whisper the secrets of life into his ears if I, shutting my doors, should try to free myself from mortal bonds?

"我的头发变白是一件小事。

"我是永远和这村里最年轻的人一样的年轻，最年老的人一样的年老。

"有的人发出甜柔单纯的微笑，有的人眼里含着狡狯的闪光。

"有的人在白天流涌着眼泪，有的人的眼泪却隐藏在幽暗里。

"他们都需要我，我没有时间去冥想来生。

"我和每一个人都是同年的，我的头发变白了又该怎样呢？"

"It is a trifle that my hair is turning grey.

"I am ever as young or as old as the youngest and the oldest of this village.

"Some have smiles, sweet and simple, and some a sly twinkle in their eyes.

"Some have tears that well up in the daylight, and others tears that are hidden in the gloom.

"They all have need for me and I have no time to brood over the afterlife.

"I am of an age with each, what matter if my hair turns grey?"

003

早晨我把网撒在海里。

我从沉黑的深渊拉出奇形奇美的东西——有些微笑般地发亮，有些眼泪般地闪光，有的晕红得像新娘的双颊。

当我携带着这一天的担负回到家里的时候，我爱正坐在园里悠闲地扯着花叶。

我沉吟了一会，就把我捞得的一切放在她的脚前，沉默地站着。

她瞥了一眼说："这是些什么怪东西？我不知道这些东西有什么用处！"

In the morning I cast my net into the sea.

I dragged up from the dark abyss things of strange aspect and strange beauty—some shone like a smile, some glistened like tears, and some were flushed like the cheeks of a bride.

When with the day's burden I went home, my love was sitting in the garden idly tearing the leaves of a flower.

I hesitated for a moment, and then placed at her feet all that I had dragged up, and stood silent.

She glanced at them and said, "What strange things are these? I know not of what use they are!"

我羞愧得低了头,心想:"我并没有为这些东西去奋斗,也不是从市场里买来的;这不是一些配送给她的礼物。"

整夜的工夫我把这些东西一件一件地丢到街上。

早晨行路的人来了;他们把这些拾起带到远方去了。

I bowed my head in shame and thought, "I have not fought for these, I did not buy them in the market; they are not fit gifts for her."

Then the whole night through I flung them one by one into the street.

In the morning travellers came; they picked them up and carried them into far countries.

004

我真烦，为什么他们把我的房子盖在通向市镇的路边呢？

他们把满载的船只拴在我的树上。

他们任意地来去游逛。

我坐着看着他们；光阴都消磨了。

我不能回绝他们。这样我的日子便过去了。

日日夜夜他们的足音在我门前震荡。

我徒然地叫道："我不认得你们。"

有些人是我的手指所认识的，有的人是我的鼻官所认识的，我脉管中的血液似乎认得他们，有些人是我的魂梦所认识的。

我不能回绝他们。我呼唤他们说："谁愿意到我房子里来就请来吧，对了，来吧。"

Ah me, why did they build my house by the road to the market town?

They moor their laden boats near my trees.

They come and go and wander at their will.

I sit and watch them; my time wears on.

Turn them away I cannot. And thus my days pass by.

Night and day their steps sound by my door.

Vainly I cry, "I do not know you."

Some of them are known to my fingers, some to my nostrils, the blood in my veins seems to know them, and some are known to my dreams.

Turn them away I cannot. I call them and say, "Come to my house whoever chooses. Yes, come."

清晨庙里的钟声敲起。

他们提着筐子来了。

他们的脚像玫瑰般红。熹微的晨光照在他们的脸上。

我不能回绝他们。我呼唤他们说："到我园里来采花吧。到这里来吧。"

In the morning the bell rings in the temple.

They come with their baskets in their hands.

Their feet are rosy-red. The early light of dawn is on their faces.

Turn them away I cannot. I call them and I say, "Come to my garden to gather flowers. Come hither."

中午锣声在庙殿门前敲起。

我不知道他们为什么放下工作在我篱畔留连。

他们发上的花朵已经褪色枯萎了；他们横笛里的音调也显得乏倦。

我不能回绝他们。我呼唤他们说："我的树荫下是凉爽的。来吧，朋友们。"

In the midday the gong sounds at the palace gate.

I know not why they leave their work and linger near my hedge.

The flowers in their hair are pale and faded; the notes are languid in their flutes.

Turn them away I cannot. I call them and say, "The shade is cool under my trees. Come, friends."

夜里蟋蟀在林中唧唧地叫。

是谁慢慢地来到我的门前轻轻地敲叩？

我模糊地看到他的脸，他一句话也没说，四围是天空的静默。

我不能回绝我的沉默的客人。我从黑暗中望着他的脸，梦幻的时间过去了。

At night the crickets chirp in the woods.

Who is it that comes slowly to my door and gently knocks?

I vaguely see the face, not a word is spoken, the stillness of the sky is all around.

Turn away my silent guest I cannot. I look at the face through the dark, and hours of dreams pass by.

005

我心绪不宁。我渴望着遥远的事物。

我的灵魂在极想中走出，要去摸触幽暗的远处的边缘。

呵，"伟大的来生"，呵，你笛声的高亢的呼唤！

我忘却了，我总是忘却了，我没有奋飞的翅翼，我永远在这地点系住。

I am restless. I am athirst for faraway things.

My soul goes out in a longing to touch the skirt of the dim distance.

O Great Beyond. O the keen call of thy flute!

I forget, I ever forget, that I have no wings to fly, that I am bound in this spot evermore.

我切望而又清醒，我是一个异乡的异客。

你的气息向我低语出一个不可能的希望。

我的心懂得你的语言就像它懂得自己的语言一样。

呵，"遥远的寻求"，呵，你笛声的高亢的呼唤！

我忘却了，我总是忘却了，我不认得路，我也没有生翼的马。

I am eager and wakeful. I am a stranger in a strange
land.

Thy breath comes to me whispering an impossible hope.

Thy tongue is known to my heart as its very own.

O Far-to-seek, O the keen call of thy flute!

I forget, I ever forget, that I know not the way, that I have
not the winged horse.

我心绪不宁。我是自己心中的流浪者。

在疲倦时光的日霭中，你广大的幻象在天空的蔚蓝中显现！

呵，"最远的尽头"，呵，你笛声的高亢的呼唤！

我忘却了，我总是忘却了，在我独居的房子里，所有的门户
都是紧闭的！

I am listless, I am a wanderer in my heart.

In the sunny haze of the languid hours, what vast vision of
thine takes shape in the blue of the sky!

O Farthest End, O the keen call of thy flute!

I forget, I ever forget, that the gates are shut everywhere in the house where I dwell alone!

006

驯养的鸟在笼里，自由的鸟在林中。

时间到了，他们相会，这是命中注定的。

自由的鸟说："呵，我爱，让我们飞到林中去吧。"

笼中的鸟低声说："到这里来吧，让我俩都住在笼里。"

自由的鸟说："在栅栏中间，哪有展翅的余地呢？"

"可怜呵，"笼中的鸟说，"在天空中我不晓得到哪里去栖息。"

The tame bird was in a cage, the free bird was in the forest.

They met when the time came, it was a decree of fate.

The free bird cries, "O my love, let us fly to wood."

The cage bird whispers, "Come hither, let us both live in the cage."

Says the free bird, "Among bars, where is there room to spread one's wings?"

"Alas," cries the cage bird, "I should not know where to sit perched in the sky."

自由的鸟叫唤说："我的宝贝，唱起林野之歌吧。"

笼中的鸟说："坐在我旁边吧，我要教你说学者的语言。"

自由的鸟叫唤说："不，不！歌曲是不能传授的。"

笼中的鸟说："可怜的我呵，我不会唱林野之歌。"

The free bird cries, "My darling, sing the songs of the woodlands."

The cage bird says, "Sit by my side. I'll teach you the speech of the learned."

The forest bird cries, "No, ah no! Songs can never be taught."

The cage bird says, "Alas for me, I know not the songs of the woodlands."

他们的爱情因渴望而更加热烈，但是他们永不能比翼双飞。

他们隔栏相望，而他们相知的愿望是虚空的。

他们在依恋中振翼，唱说："靠近些吧，我爱！"

自由的鸟叫唤说："这是做不到的，我怕这笼子的紧闭的门。"

笼里的鸟低声说："我的翅翼是无力的，而且已经死去了。"

Their love is intense with longing, but they never can fly

wing to wing.

Through the bars of the cage they look, and vain is their wish to know each other.

They flutter their wings in yearning, and sing, "Come closer, my love!"

The free bird cries, "It cannot be, I fear the closed doors of the cage."

The cage bird whispers, "Alas, my wings are powerless and dead."

007

呵，母亲，年轻的王子要从我们门前走过，——今天早晨我哪有心思干活呢？

教给我怎样挽发；告诉我应该穿哪件衣裳。

你为什么惊讶地望着我呢，母亲？

我深知他不会仰视我的窗户；我知道一刹那间他就要走出我的视线以外；只有那残曳的笛声将从远处向我呜咽。

但是那年轻的王子将从我们门前走过，这时节我要穿上我最好的衣裳。

O mother, the young Prince is to pass by our door,—how can I attend to my work this morning?

Show me how to braid up my hair; tell me what garment to put on.

Why do you look at me amazed, mother?

I know well he will not glance up once at my window; I know he will pass out of my sight in the twinkling of an eye; only the vanishing strain of the flute will come sobbing to me from afar.

But the young Prince will pass by our door, and I will put on my best for the moment.

呵，母亲，年轻的王子已经从我们门前走过了，从他的车辇里射出朝日的金光。

我从脸上掠开面纱，我从颈上扯下红玉的颈环，扔在他走来的路上。

你为什么惊讶地望着我呢，母亲？

我深知他没有拾起我的颈环；我知道它在他的轮下碾碎了，在尘土上留下了红斑，没有人晓得我的礼物是什么样子，也不知道是给谁的。

但是那年轻的王子曾经从我们门前走过，我也曾经把我胸前的珍宝丢在他走来的路上了。

O mother, the young Prince did pass by our door, and the morning sun flashed from his chariot.

I swept aside the veil from my face, I tore the ruby chain from my neck and flung it in his path.

Why do you look at me amazed, mother?

I know well he did not pick up my chain, I know it was crushed under his wheels leaving a red stain upon the dust, and no one knows what my gift was nor to whom.

But the young Prince did pass by our door, and I flung the jewel from my breast before his path.

008

当我床前的灯熄灭了，我和晨鸟一同醒起。

我在散发上戴上新鲜的花串，坐在洞开的窗前。

那年轻的行人在玫瑰色的朝霞中从大路上来了。

珠链在他的颈上，阳光在他的冠上。他停在我的门前，用切望的呼声问我，"她在哪里呢？"

为着深羞我说不出："她就是我，年轻的行人，她就是我。"

When the lamp went out by my bed I woke up with the early birds.

I sat at my open window with a fresh wreath on my loose hair.

The young traveller came along the road in the rosy mist of the morning.

A pearl chain was on his neck and the sun's rays fell on his crown. He stopped before my door and asked me with an eager cry, "Where is she?"

For very shame I could not say, "She is I, young traveller, she is I."

黄昏来到，还未上灯。

我心绪不宁地编着头发。

在落日的光辉中年轻的行人驾着车辇来了。

他的驾车的马，嘴里喷着白沫，他的衣袍上蒙着尘土。

他在我的门前下车，用疲乏的声音问，"她在哪里呢？"

为着深羞我说不出："她就是我，愁倦的行人，她就是我。"

It was dusk and the lamp was not lit.

I was listlessly braiding my hair.

The young traveller came on his chariot in the glow of the setting sun.

His horses were foaming at the mouth, and there was dust on his garment.

He alighted at my door and asked in a tired voice, "Where is she?"

For very shame I could not say, "She is I, weary traveller, she is I."

一个四月的夜晚。我的屋里点着灯。

南风温柔地吹来。多言的鹦鹉在笼里睡着了。

我的衷衣 ① 和孔雀颈毛一样地华彩，我的披纱和嫩草一样地碧青。

我坐在窗前地上看望着冷落的街道。

在沉黑的夜中我不住地低吟着："她就是我，失望的行人，她就是我。"

It is an April night. The lamp is burning in my room.

The breeze of the south comes gently. The noisy parrot sleeps in its cage.

My bodice is of the colour of the peacock's throat, and my mantle is green as young grass.

I sit upon the floor at the window watching the deserted street.

Through the dark night I keep humming, "She is I, despairing traveller, she is I."

---

① 衷衣：贴身内衣。

009

当我在夜中独赴幽会的时候，鸟儿不叫，风儿不吹，街道两旁的房屋沉默地站立着。

是我自己的脚镯越走越响使我羞怯。

When I go alone at night to my love-tryst, birds do not sing, the wind does not stir, the houses on both sides of the street stand silent.

It is my own anklets that grow loud at every step and I am ashamed.

当我坐在凉台上倾听他的足音，树叶不摇，河水静止像熟睡的哨兵膝上的刀剑。

是我自己的心在狂跳——我不知道怎样使它宁静。

When I sit on my balcony and listen for his footsteps,

leaves do not rustle on the trees, and the water is still in the river like the sword on the knees of a sentry fallen asleep.

It is my own heart that beats wildly—I do not know how to quiet it.

当我爱来了，坐在我身旁，当我的身躯震颤，我的眼睫下垂，夜更深了，风吹灯灭，云片在繁星上曳过轻纱。

是我自己胸前的珍宝放出光明。我不知道怎样把它遮起。

When my love comes and sits by my side, when my body trembles and my eyelids droop, the night darkens, the wind blows out the lamp, and the clouds draw veils over the stars.

It is the jewel at my own breast that shines and gives light. I do not know how to hide it.

010

放下你的工作吧，我的新娘。听，客人来了。

你听见没有，他在轻轻地摇动那拴门的链子?

小心不要让你的脚镯响出声音，在迎接他的时候你的脚步不要太急。

放下你的工作吧，新娘，客人在晚上来了。

Let your work be, bride. Listen, the guest has come.

Do you hear, he is gently shaking the chain which fastens the door?

See that your anklets make no loud noise, and that your step is not over-hurried at meeting him.

Let your work be, bride, the guest has come in the evening.

不，这不是一阵阴风，新娘，不要惊惶。

这是四月夜中的满月；院里的影子是暗淡的；头上的天空是明亮的。

把轻纱遮上脸，若是你觉得需要；提着灯到门前去，若是你害怕。

No, it is not the ghostly wind, bride, do not be frightened.

It is the full moon on a night of April; shadows are pale in the courtyard; the sky overhead is bright.

Draw your veil over your face if you must, carry the lamp to the door if you fear.

不，这不是一阵阴风，新娘，不要惊惶。

若是你害羞就不必和他说话；你迎接他的时候只须站在门边。

No, it is not the ghostly wind, bride, do not be frightened.

Have no word with him if you are shy; stand aside by the door when you meet him.

他若问你话，若是你愿意这样做，你就沉默地低眸。

不要让你的手镯作响，当我提着灯，带他进来的时候。

不必同他说话，如果你害羞。

If he asks you questions, and if you wish to, you can lower your eyes in silence.

Do not let your bracelets jingle when, lamp in hand, you lead him in.

Have no word with him if you are shy.

你的工作还没有做完么，新娘？听，客人来了。

你还没有把牛棚里的灯点起来么？

你还没有把晚祷的供筐准备好么？

你还没有在发缝中涂上鲜红的吉祥点，你还没有理过晚妆么？

呵，新娘，你没有听见，客人来了么？

放下你的工作吧。

Have you not finished your work yet, bride? Listen, the guest has come.

Have you not lit the lamp in the cowshed?

Have you not got ready the offering-basket for the evening service?

Have you not put the red lucky mark at the parting of your hair, and done your toilet for the night?

O bride, do you hear, the guest has come?

Let your work be!

011

你就这样地来吧；不要在梳妆上换延了。

即使你的鬈发松散，即使你的发鬈没有分直，即使你衷衣的丝带没有系好，都不要管它。

你就这样地来吧；不要在梳妆上换延了。

Come as you are; do not loiter over your toilet.

If your braided hair has loosened, if the parting of your hair be not straight, if the ribbons of your bodice be not fastened, do not mind.

Come as you are, do not loiter over your toilet.

来吧，用快步踏过草坪。

即使露水沾掉了你脚上的红粉，即使你踝上的铃串褪松，即使你链上的珠儿脱落，都不要管它。

来吧，用快步踏过草坪吧。

Come, with quick steps over the grass.

If the raddle come from your feet because of the dew, if the rings of bells upon your feet slacken, if pearls drop out of your chain, do not mind.

Come, with quick steps over the grass.

你没看见云雾遮住天空么？

鹤群从远远的河岸飞起，狂风吹过常青的灌木。

惊牛奔向村里的栅棚。

你没看见云雾遮住天空么？

Do you see the clouds wrapping the sky?

Flocks of cranes fly up from the further river-bank and fitful gusts of wind rush over the heath.

The anxious cattle run to their stalls in the village.

Do you see the clouds wrapping the sky?

你徒然点上晚妆的灯火——它颤摇着在风中熄灭了。

谁能看出你眼睫上没有涂上乌烟？因为你的眼睛比雨云还黑。

你徒然点上晚妆的灯火——它熄灭了。

In vain you light your toilet lamp—it flickers and goes out in the wind.

Who can know that your eyelids have not been touched with lampblack? For your eyes are darker than rain-clouds.

In vain you light your toilet lamp—it goes out.

你就这样地来吧，不要在梳妆上挨延了。

即使花环没有穿好，谁管它呢；即使手镯没有扣上，让它去吧。

天空被阴云塞满了——时间已晚。

你就这样地来吧；不要在梳妆上挨延了。

Come as you are; do not loiter over your toilet.

If the wreath is not woven, who cares; if the wrist-chain has not been linked, let it be.

The sky is overcast with clouds—it is late.

Come as you are; do not loiter over your toilet.

012

若是你要忙着把水瓶灌满，来吧，到我的湖上来吧。

湖水将回绕在你的脚边，潺潺地说出它的秘密。

沙滩上有了欲来的雨云的阴影，云雾低垂在丛树的绿线上，像你眉上的浓发。

我深深地熟悉你脚步的韵律，它在我心中敲击。

来吧，到我的湖上来吧，如果你必须把水瓶灌满。

If you would be busy and fill your pitcher, come, O come to my lake.

The water will cling round your feet and babble its secret.

The shadow of the coming rain is on the sands, and the clouds hang low upon the blue lines of the trees like the heavy hair above your eyebrows.

I know well the rhythm of your steps, they are beating in my heart.

Come, O come to my lake, if you must fill your pitcher.

如果你想懒散闲坐，让你的水瓶漂浮在水面，来吧，到我的湖上来吧。

草坡碧绿，野花多得数不清。

你的思想将从你乌黑的眼眸中飞出，像鸟儿飞出窝巢。

你的披纱将褪落到脚上。

来吧，如果你要闲坐，到我的湖上来吧。

If you would be idle and sit listless and let your pitcher float on the water, come, O come to my lake.

The grassy slope is green, and the wild flowers beyond number.

Your thoughts will stray out of your dark eyes like birds from their nests.

Your veil will drop to your feet.

Come, O come to my lake if you must sit idle.

如果你想撇下嬉游跳进水里，来吧，到我的湖上来吧。

把你的蔚蓝的丝巾留在岸上；蔚蓝的水将没过你，盖住你。

水波将蹑足来吻你的颈项，在你耳边低语。

来吧，如果你想跳进水里，到我的湖上来吧。

If you would leave off your play and dive in the water, come, O come to my lake.

Let your blue mantle lie on the shore; the blue water will cover you and hide you.

The waves will stand a-tiptoe to kiss your neck and whisper in your ears.

Come, O come to my lake, if you would dive in the water.

如果你想发狂而投入死亡，来吧，到我的湖上来吧。
它是清凉的，深到无底。
它沉黑得像无梦的睡眠。
在它的深处黑夜就是白天，歌曲就是静默。
来吧，如果你想投入死亡，到我的湖上来吧。

If you must be mad and leap to your death, come, O come to my lake.

It is cool and fathomlessly deep.

It is dark like a sleep that is dreamless.

There in its depths nights and days are one, and songs are silence.

Come, O come to my lake, if you would plunge to your death.

013

我一无所求，只站在林边树后。

倦意还逗留在黎明的眼上，露润在空气里。

湿草的懒味悬垂在地面的薄雾中。

在榕树下你用乳油般柔嫩的手挤着牛奶。

我沉静地站立着。

I asked nothing, only stood at the edge of the wood behind the tree.

Languor was still upon the eyes of the dawn, and the dew in the air.

The lazy smell of the damp grass hung in the thin mist above the earth.

Under the banyan tree you were milking the cow with your hands, tender and fresh as butter.

And I was standing still.

我没有说出一个字。那是藏起的鸟儿在密叶中歌唱。

芒果树在村径上撒着繁花，蜜蜂一只一只地嗡嗡飞来。

池塘边湿婆天的庙门开了，朝拜者开始诵经。

你把罐儿放在膝上挤着牛奶。

我提着空桶站立着。

I did not say a word. It was the bird that sang unseen from the thicket.

The mango tree was shedding its flowers upon the village road, and the bees came humming one by one.

On the side of the pond the gate of Shiva's temple was opened and the worshipper had begun his chants.

With the vessel on your lap you were milking the cow.

I stood with my empty can.

我没有走近你。

天空和庙里的锣声一同醒起。

街尘在驱走的牛蹄下飞扬。

把汩汩发响的水瓶搂在腰上，女人们从河边走来。

你的钏镯叮当，乳沫溢出罐沿。

晨光渐逝而我没有走近你。

I did not come near you.

The sky woke with the sound of the gong at the temple.

The dust was raised in the road from the hoofs of the driven cattle.

With the gurgling pitchers at their hips, women came from the river.

Your bracelets were jingling, and foam brimming over the jar.

The morning wore on and I did not come near you.

014

我在路边行走，也不知道为什么，
时已过午，竹枝在风中簌簌作响。
横斜的影子伸臂拖住流光的双足。
布谷鸟都唱倦了。
我在路边行走，也不知道为什么。

I was walking by the road, I do not know why,
    when the noonday was past and bamboo branches
rustled in the wind.
    The prone shadows with their outstretched arms clung to
the feet of the hurrying light.
    The koels were weary of their songs.
    I was walking by the road, I do not know why.

低垂的树荫盖住水边的茅屋。

有人正忙着工作，她的钏镯在一角放出音乐。

我在茅屋前面站着，我不知道为什么。

The hut by the side of the water is shaded by an overhanging tree.

Some one was busy with her work, and her bangles made music in the corner.

I stood before this hut, I know not why.

曲径穿过一片芥菜田地和几层芒果树林。

它经过村庙和渡头的市集。

我在这茅屋面前停住了，我不知道为什么。

The narrow winding road crosses many a mustard field, and many a mango forest.

It passes by the temple of the village and the market at the river landing-place.

I stopped by this hut, I do not know why.

好几年前，三月风吹的一天，春天倦慵地低语，芒果花落在地上。

浪花跳起掠过立在渡头阶沿上的铜瓶。

我想着三月风吹的这一天，我不知道为什么。

Years ago it was a day of breezy March when the murmur of the spring was languorous, and mango blossoms were dropping on the dust.

The rippling water leapt and licked the brass vessel that stood on the landing-step.

I think of that day of breezy March, I do not know why.

阴影更深，牛群归栏。

冷落的牧场上日色苍白，村人在河边待渡。

我缓步回去，我不知道为什么。

Shadows are deepening and cattle returning to their folds.

The light is grey upon the lonely meadows, and the villagers are waiting for the ferry at the bank.

I slowly return upon my steps, I do not know why.

015

我像麝鹿一样在林荫中奔走，为着自己的香气而发狂。

夜晚是五月正中的夜晚，清风是南国的清风。

我迷了路，我游荡着，我寻求那得不到的东西，我得到我所没有寻求的东西。

I run as a musk-deer runs in the shadow of the forest mad with his own perfume.

The night is the night of mid-May, the breeze is the breeze of the south.

I lose my way and I wander, I seek what I cannot get, I get what I do not seek.

我自己的愿望的形象从我心中走出，跳起舞来。

我闪光的形象飞掠过去。

我想把它紧紧捉住，它躲开了又引着我飞走下去。

我寻求那得不到的东西，我得到我所没有寻求的东西。

From my heart comes out and dances the image of my own desire.

The gleaming vision flits on.

I try to clasp it firmly, it eludes me and leads me astray.

I seek what I cannot get, I get what I do not seek.

016

手握着手，眼恋着眼：这样开始了我们的心的纪录。

这是三月的月明之夜；空气里有凤仙花的芬芳；我的横笛抛在地上，你的花串也没有编成。

你我之间的爱像歌曲一样地单纯。

Hands cling to hands and eyes linger on eyes: thus begins the record of our hearts.

It is the moonlit night of March; the sweet smell of henna is in the air; my flute lies on the earth neglected and your garland of flowers is unfinished.

This love between you and me is simple as a song.

你橙黄色的面纱使我眼睛陶醉。

你给我编的茉莉花环使我心震颤，像是受了赞扬。

这是一个又予又留，又隐又现的游戏；有些微笑，有些娇羞，也有些甜柔的无用的抵拦。

你我之间的爱像歌曲一样地单纯。

Your veil of the saffron colour makes my eyes drunk.

The jasmine wreath that you wove me thrills to my heart like praise.

It is a game of giving and withholding, revealing and screening again; some smiles and some little shyness, and some sweet useless struggles.

This love between you and me is simple as a song.

没有现在以外的神秘；不强求那做不到的事情；没有魅惑后面的阴影；没有黑暗深处的探索。

你我之间的爱像歌曲一样地单纯。

No mystery beyond the present; no striving for the impossible; no shadow behind the charm; no groping in the depth of the dark.

This love between you and me is simple as a song.

我们没有走出一切语言之外进入永远的沉默；我们没有向空举手寻求希望以外的东西。

　　我们付与，我们取得，这就够了。

　　我们没有把喜乐压成微尘来榨取痛苦之酒。

　　你我之间的爱像歌曲一样地单纯。

　　We do not stray out of all words into the ever silent; we do not raise our hands to the void for things beyond hope.

　　It is enough what we give and we get.

　　We have not crushed the joy to the utmost to wring from it the wine of pain.

　　This love between you and me is simple as a song.

017

黄鸟在自己的树上歌唱，使我的心喜舞。

我们两人住在一个村子里，这是我们的一份快乐。

她心爱的一对小羊，到我园树的荫下吃草。

它们若走进我的麦地，我就把它们抱在臂里。

我们村子名叫康遮那，人们管我们的小河叫安遮那。

我的名字村人都知道，她的名字是软遮那。

The yellow bird sings in their tree and makes my heart dance with gladness.

We both live in the same village, and that is our one piece of joy.

Her pair of pet lambs come to graze in the shade of our garden trees.

If they stray into our barley field, I take them up in my arms.

The name of our village is Khanjanā, and Anjanā they call our river.

My name is known to all the village, and her name is
Ranjanā.

我们中间只隔着一块田地。

在我们树里做窝的蜜蜂，飞到他们林中去采蜜。

从他们渡头阶上流来的落花，飘到我们洗澡的池塘里。

一筐一筐的红花干从他们地里送到我们的市集上。

我们村子名叫康遮那，人们管我们的小河叫安遮那。

我的名字村人都知道，她的名字是软遮那。

Only one field lies between us.

Bees that have hived in our grove go to seek honey in
theirs.

Flowers launched from their landing-stairs come floating
by the stream where we bathe.

Baskets of dried kuṣm flowers come from their fields to our
market.

The name of our village is Khanjanā, and Anjanā they call
our river.

My name is known to all the village, and her name is
Ranjanā.

到她家去的那条曲巷，春天充满了芒果的花香。

他们亚麻子成熟的时候，我们地里的大麻正在开放。

在他们房上微笑的星辰，送给我们以同样的闪亮。

在他们水槽里满溢的雨水，也使我们的迦昙树林喜乐。

我们村子名叫康遮那，人们管我们的小河叫安遮那。

我的名字村人都知道，她的名字是软遮那。

The lane that winds to their house is fragrant in the spring with mango flowers.

When their linseed is ripe for harvest the hemp is in bloom in our field.

The stars that smile on their cottage send us the same twinkling look.

The rain that floods their tank makes glad our kadam forest.

The name of our village is Khanjanā, and Anjanā they call our river.

My name is known to all the village, and her name is Ranjanā.

018

当这两个姊妹出去打水的时候，她们来到这地点，她们微笑了。

她们一定觉察到，每次她们出来打水的时候，那个站在树后的人儿。

When the two sisters go to fetch water, they come to this spot and they smile.

They must be aware of somebody who stands behind the trees whenever they go to fetch water.

姊妹俩相互耳语，当她们走到这地点的时候。

她们一定猜到了，每逢她们出来打水的时候，那个人站在树后的秘密。

The two sisters whisper to each other when they pass this

spot.

They must have guessed the secret of that somebody who stands behind the trees whenever they go to fetch water.

她们的水瓶忽然倾倒，水倒出来了，当她们走到这地点的时候。

她们一定发觉，每逢她们出来打水的时候，那个站在树后的人的心正在跳着。

Their pitchers lurch suddenly, and water spills when they reach this spot.

They must have found out that somebody's heart is beating who stands behind the trees whenever they go to fetch water.

姊妹俩相互瞥了一眼又微笑了，当她们来到这地点的时候。

她们飞快的脚步里带着笑声，使这个每逢她们出来打水的时候站在树后的人儿心魂撩乱了。

The two sisters glance at each other when they come to this spot, and they smile.

There is a laughter in their swift-stepping feet, which makes confusion in somebody's mind who stands behind the trees whenever they go to fetch water.

019

你腰间搂着灌满的水瓶，在河边路上行走。

你为什么急遽地回头，从飘扬的面纱里偷偷地看我？

这个从黑暗中向我送来的闪视，像凉风在粼粼的微波上掠过，一阵震颤直到阴荫的岸边。

它向我飞来，像夜中的小鸟急遽地穿过无灯的屋子的两边洞开的窗户，又在黑夜中消失了。

你像一颗隐在山后的星星，我是路上的行人。

但是你为什么站了一会，从面纱中瞥视我的脸，当你腰间搂着灌满的水瓶在河边路上行走的时候？

You walked by the riverside path with the full pitcher upon your hip.

Why did you swiftly turn your face and peep at me through your fluttering veil?

That gleaming look from the dark came upon me like a breeze that sends a shiver through the rippling water and sweeps away to the shadowy shore.

It came to me like the bird of the evening that hurriedly

flies across the lampless room from the one open window to the other, and disappears in the night.

You are hidden as a star behind the hills, and I am a passer-by upon the road.

But why did you stop for a moment and glance at my face through your veil while you walked by the riverside path with the full pitcher upon your hip?

020

他天天来了又走了。

去吧，把我头上的花朵送去给他吧，我的朋友。

假如他问赠花的人是谁，我请你不要把我的名字告诉他——因为他来了又要走的。

Day after day he comes and goes away.

Go, and give him a flower from my hair, my friend.

If he asks who was it that sent it, I entreat you do not tell him my name—for he only comes and goes away.

他坐在树下的地上。

用繁花密叶给他敷设一个座位吧，我的朋友。

他的眼神是忧郁的，它把忧郁带到我的心中。

他没有说出他的心事；他只是来了又走了。

He sits on the dust under the tree.

Spread there a seat with flowers and leaves, my friend.

His eyes are sad, and they bring sadness to my heart.

He does not speak what he has in mind; he only comes and goes away.

021

他为什么特地来到我的门前，这年轻的游子，当天色黎明的时候?

每次我进出经过他的身旁，我的眼睛总被他的面庞所吸引。

我不知道我是应该同他说话还是保持沉默。他为什么特地到我门前来呢?

Why did he choose to come to my door, the wandering youth, when the day dawned?

As I come in and out I pass by him every time, and my eyes are caught by his face.

I know not if I should speak to him or keep silent. Why did he choose to come to my door?

七月的阴夜是黑沉的;秋日的天空是浅蓝的;南风把春天吹得骀荡不宁。

他每次用新调编着新歌。

我放下活计眼里充满雾水。他为什么特地到我门前来呢?

The cloudy nights in July are dark; the sky is soft blue in the autumn; the spring days are restless with the south wind.

He weaves his songs with fresh tunes every time.

I turn from my work and my eyes fill with the mist. Why did he choose to come to my door?

022

当她用急步走过我的身旁，她的裙缘触到了我。

从一颗心的无名小岛上忽然吹来一阵春天的温馨。

一霎飞触的撩乱扫拂过我，立刻又消失了，像扯落的花瓣在和风中飘扬。

它落在我的心上，像她的身躯的叹息和她的心灵的低语。

When she passed by me with quick steps, the end of her skirt touched me.

From the unknown island of a heart came a sudden warm breath of spring.

A flutter of a flitting touch brushed me and vanished in a moment, like a torn flower petal blown in the breeze.

It fell upon my heart like a sigh of her body and whisper of her heart.

023

你为什么悠闲地坐在那里，把镯子玩得叮当作响呢？
把你的水瓶灌满了吧。是你应当回家的时候了。

Why do you sit there and jingle your bracelets in mere idle sport?

Fill your pitcher. It is time for you to come home.

你为什么悠闲地拨弄着水玩，偷偷地瞥视路上的行人呢？
灌满你的水瓶回家去吧。

Why do you stir the water with your hands and fitfully glance at the road for some one in mere idle sport?

Fill your pitcher and come home.

早晨的时间过去了——沉黑的水不住地流逝。

波浪相互低语嬉笑闲玩着。

The morning hours pass by—the dark water flows on.

The waves are laughing and whispering to each other in mere idle sport.

流荡的云片聚集在远野高地的天边。

它们留连着悠闲地看着你的脸微笑着。

灌满你的水瓶回家去吧。

The wandering clouds have gathered at the edge of the sky on yonder rise of the land.

They linger and look at your face and smile in mere idle sport.

Fill your pitcher and come home.

024

不要把你心的秘密藏起，我的朋友！

对我说吧，秘密地对我一个人说吧。

你这个笑得这样温柔，说得这样轻软的人，我的心将听着你的语言，不是我的耳朵。

夜深沉，庭宁静，鸟巢也被睡眠笼罩着。

从踌躇的眼泪里，从沉吟的微笑里，从甜柔的羞怯和痛苦里，把你心的秘密告诉我吧！

Do not keep to yourself the secret of your heart, my friend!

Say it to me, only to me, in secret.

You who smile so gently, softly whisper, my heart will hear it, not my ears.

The night is deep, the house is silent, the birds'nests are shrouded with sleep.

Speak to me through hesitating tears, through faltering smiles, through sweet shame and pain, the secret of your heart!

025

"到我们这里来吧，青年人，老实告诉我们，为什么你眼里带着疯癫？"

"我不知道我喝了什么野罂粟花酒，使我的眼里带着疯癫。"

"呵，多难为情！"

"好吧，有的人聪明有的人愚拙，有的人细心有的人马虎。有的眼睛会笑，有的眼睛会哭——我的眼睛是带着疯癫的。"

"Come to us, youth, tell us truly why there is madness in your eyes?"

"I know not what wine of wild poppy I have drunk, that there is this madness in my eyes."

"Ah, shame!"

"Well, some are wise and some foolish, some are watchful and some careless. There are eyes that smile and eyes that weep—and madness is in my eyes."

"青年人，你为什么这样凝立在树影下呢？"

"我的脚被我沉重的心压得疲倦了，我就在树影下凝立着。"

"呵，多难为情！"

"好吧，有人一直行进，有人到处留连，有的人是自由的，有的人是锁住的——我的脚被我沉重的心压得疲倦了。"

"Youth, why do you stand so still under the shadow of the tree?"

"My feet are languid with the burden of my heart, and I stand still in the shadow."

"Ah, shame!"

"Well, some march on their way and some linger, some are free and some are fettered—and my feet are languid with the burden of my heart."

026

"从你慷慨的手里所付予的我都接受。我别无所求。"

"是了，是了，我懂得你，谦卑的乞丐，你是乞求一个人的一切所有。"

"What comes from your willing hands I take. I beg for nothing more."

"Yes, yes, I know you, modest mendicant, you ask for all that one has."

"若是你给我一朵残花，我也要把它戴在心上。"

"若是那花上有刺呢？"

"我就忍受着。"

"是了，是了，我懂得你，谦卑的乞丐，你是乞求一个人的一切所有。"

"If there be a stray flower for me I will wear it in my heart."

"But if there be thorns?"

"I will endure them."

"Yes, yes, I know you, modest mendicant, you ask for all that one has."

"如果你只在我脸上瞥来一次爱怜的眼光，就会使我的生命直到死后还是甜蜜的。"

"假如那只是残酷的眼色呢？"

"我要让它永远穿刺我的心。"

"是了，是了，我懂得你，谦卑的乞丐，你是乞求一个人的一切所有。"

"If but once you should raise your loving eyes to my face it would make my life sweet beyond death."

"But if there be only cruel glances?"

"I will keep them piercing my heart."

"Yes, yes, I know you, modest mendicant, you ask for all that one has."

027

"即使爱只给你带来了哀愁，也信任它。不要把你的心关起。"

"呵，不，我的朋友，你的话语太隐晦了，我不懂得。"

"Trust love even if it brings sorrow. Do not close up your heart."

"Ah, no, my friend, your words are dark, I cannot understand them."

"心是应该和一滴眼泪，一首诗歌一起送给人的，我爱。"

"呵，不，我的朋友，你的话语太隐晦了，我不懂得。"

"The heart is only for giving away with a tear and a song, my love."

"Ah, no, my friend, your words are dark, I cannot understand them."

"喜乐像露珠一样地脆弱，它在欢笑中死去。哀愁却是坚强而耐久。让含愁的爱在你眼中醒起吧。"

"呵，不，我的朋友，你的话语太隐晦了，我不懂得。"

"Pleasure is frail like a dewdrop, while it laughs it dies. But sorrow is strong and abiding. Let sorrowful love wake in your eyes."

"Ah, no, my friend, your words are dark, I cannot understand them."

"荷花在日中开放，丢掉了自己的一切所有。在永生的冬雾里，它将不再含苞。"

"呵，不，我的朋友，你的话语太隐晦了，我不懂得。"

"The lotus blooms in the sight of the sun, and loses all that it has. It would not remain in bud in the eternal winter mist."

"Ah, no, my friend, your words are dark, I cannot understand them."

028

你的疑问的眼光是含愁的。它要追探了解我的意思，好像月亮探测大海。

我已经把我生命的终始，全部暴露在你的眼前，没有任何隐秘和保留。因此你不认识我。

假如它是一块宝石，我就能把它碎成千百颗粒，穿成项链挂在你的颈上。

假如它是一朵花，圆圆小小香香的，我就能从枝上采来戴在你的发上。

但是它是一颗心，我的爱人。何处是它的边和底？

你不知道这个王国的边极，但你仍是这王国的女王。

假如它是片刻的欢愉，它将在喜笑中开花，你立刻就会看到、懂得了。

假如它是一阵痛苦，它将融化成晶莹的眼泪，不着一字地反映出它最深的秘密。

但是它是爱，我的爱人。

它的欢乐和痛苦是无边的，它的需求和财富是无尽的。

它和你亲近得像你的生命一样，但是你永远不能完全了解它。

Your questioning eyes are sad. They seek to know my meaning as the moon would fathom the sea.

I have bared my life before your eyes from end to end, with nothing hidden or held back. That is why you know me not.

If it were only a gem, I could break it into a hundred pieces and string them into a chain to put on your neck.

If it were only a flower, round and small and sweet, I could pluck it from its stem to set it in your hair.

But it is a heart, my beloved. Where are its shores and its bottom?

You know not the limits of this kingdom, still you are its queen.

If it were only a moment of pleasure it would flower in an easy smile, and you could see it and read it in a moment.

If it were merely a pain it would melt in limpid tears, reflecting its inmost secret without a word.

But it is love, my beloved.

Its pleasure and pain are boundless, and endless its wants and wealth.

It is as near to you as your life, but you can never wholly know it.

029

对我说吧，我爱！用言语告诉我你唱的是什么。

夜是深黑的，星星消失在云里，风在叶丛中叹息。

我将披散我的头发，我的青蓝的披风将像黑夜一样地紧裹着我。我将把你的头紧抱在胸前；在甜柔的寂寞中在你心头低诉。我将闭目静听。我不会看望你的脸。

等到你的话说完了，我们将沉默凝坐。只有丛树在黑暗中微语。

夜将发白。天光将晓。我们将望望彼此的眼睛，然后各走各的路。

对我说话吧，我爱！用言语告诉我你唱的是什么。

Speak to me, my love! Tell me in words what you sang.

The night is dark. The stars are lost in clouds. The wind is sighing through the leaves.

I will let loose my hair. My blue cloak will cling round me like night. I will clasp your head to my bosom; and there in the sweet loneliness murmur on your heart. I will shut my eyes and listen. I will not look in your face.

When your words are ended, we will sit still and silent. Only the trees will whisper in the dark.

The night will pale. The day will dawn. We shall look at each other's eyes and go on our different paths.

Speak to me, my love! Tell me in words what you sang.

030

你是一朵夜云，在我梦幻中的天空中浮泛。

我永远用爱恋的渴想来描画你。

你是我一个人的，我一个人的，我无尽的梦幻中的居住者！

You are the evening cloud floating in the sky of my dreams.

I paint you and fashion you ever with my love longings.

You are my own, my own. Dweller in my endless dreams!

你的双脚被我心切望的热光染得绯红，我的落日之歌的搜集者！

我的痛苦之酒使你的唇儿苦甜。

你是我一个人的，我一个人的，我寂寥的梦幻中的居住者！

Your feet are rosy-red with the glow of my heart's desire. Gleaner of my sunset songs!

Your lips are bitter-sweet with the taste of my wine of

pain.

You are my own, my own. Dweller in my lonesome dreams!

我用热情的浓影染黑了你的眼睛，我的凝视深处的崇魂！

我捉住了你，缠住了你，我爱，在我音乐的罗网里。

你是我一个人的，我一个人的，我永生的梦幻中的居住者！

With the shadow of my passion have I darkened your eyes, Haunter of the depth of my gaze!

I have caught you and wrapt you, my love, in the net of my music.

You are my own, my own. Dweller in my deathless dreams!

031

我的心，这只野鸟，在你的双眼中找到了天空。

它们是清晓的摇篮，它们是星辰的王国。

我的诗歌在它们的深处消失。

只让我在这天空中高飞，翱翔在静寂的无限空间里。

只让我冲破它的云层，在它的阳光中展翅吧。

My heart, the bird of the wilderness, has found its sky in your eyes.

They are the cradle of the morning, they are the kingdom of the stars.

My songs are lost in their depths.

Let me but soar in that sky, in its lonely immensity.

Let me but cleave its clouds and spread wings in its sunshine.

032

告诉我，这一切是否都是真的，我的情人，告诉我，这是否真的。

当这一对眼睛闪出电光，你胸中的浓云发出风暴的回答。

我的唇儿，是真像觉醒的初恋的蓓蕾那样香甜么？

消失了的五月的回忆仍旧留连在我的肢体上么？

那大地，像一张琴，真因着我双足的踏触而颤成诗歌么？

那么当我来时，从夜的眼睛里真的落下露珠，晨光也真因为围绕我的身躯而感到喜悦么？

是真的么，是真的么，你的爱贯穿许多时代许多世界来寻找我么？

当你最后找到了我，你天长地久的渴望，在我的温柔的话里，在我的眼睛嘴唇和飘扬的头发里，找到了完全的宁静么？

那么"无限"的神秘是真的写在我小小的额上么？

告诉我，我的情人，这一切是否都是真的。

Tell me if this be all true, my lover, tell me if this be true.

When these eyes flash their lightning the dark clouds in your breast make stormy answer.

Is it true that my lips are sweet like the opening bud of the first conscious love?

Do the memories of vanished months of May linger in my limbs?

Does the earth, like a harp, shiver into songs with the touch of my feet?

Is it then true that the dewdrops fall from the eyes of night when I am seen, and the morning light is glad when it wraps my body round?

Is it true, is it true, that your love travelled alone through ages and worlds in search of me?

That when you found me at last, your agelong desire found utter peace in my gentle speech and my eyes and lips and flowing hair?

Is it then true that the mystery of the Infinite is written on this little forehead of mine?

Tell me, my lover, if all this be true.

033

我爱你，我的爱人。请饶恕我的爱。

像一只迷路的鸟，我被捉住了。

当我的心抖战的时候，它丢了围纱，变成赤裸。用怜悯遮住它吧。爱人，请饶恕我的爱。

I love you, beloved. Forgive me my love.

Like a bird losing its way I am caught.

When my heart was shaken it lost its veil and was naked. Cover it with pity, beloved, and forgive me my love.

如果你不能爱我，爱人，请饶恕我的痛苦。

不要远远地斜视我。

我将偷偷地回到我的角落里去，在黑暗中坐地。

我将用双手掩起我赤裸的羞惭。

回过脸去吧，我的爱人，请饶恕我的痛苦。

If you cannot love me, beloved, forgive me my pain.

Do not look askance at me from afar.

I will steal back to my corner and sit in the dark.

With both hands I will cover my naked shame.

Turn your face from me, beloved, and forgive me my pain.

如果你爱我，爱人，请饶恕我的欢乐。

当我的心被快乐的洪水卷走的时候，不要笑我的汹涌的退却。

当我坐在宝座上，用我暴虐的爱来统治你的时候，当我像女神一样向你施恩的时候，饶恕我的骄傲吧，爱人，也饶恕我的快乐。

If you love me, beloved, forgive me my joy.

When my heart is borne away by the flood of happiness, do not smile at my perilous abandonment.

When I sit on my throne and rule you with my tyranny of love, when like a goddess I grant you my favour, bear with my pride, beloved, and forgive me my joy.

034

不要不辞而别，我爱。

我看望了一夜，现在我眼上睡意重重。

只恐我在睡中把你丢失了。

不要不辞而别，我爱。

Do not go, my love, without asking my leave.

I have watched all night, and now my eyes are heavy with sleep.

I fear lest I lose you when I am sleeping.

Do not go, my love, without asking my leave.

我惊起伸出双手去摸触你，我问自己说："这是一个梦么？"

但愿我能用我的心系住你的双足，紧抱在胸前！

不要不辞而别，我爱。

I start up and stretch my hands to touch you. I ask myself,
"Is it a dream?"

Could I but entangle your feet with my heart and hold
them fast to my breast!

Do not go, my love, without asking my leave.

035

只恐我太容易地认得你，你对我耍花招。

你用欢笑的闪光使我目盲来掩盖你的眼泪。

我知道，我知道你的妙计，

你从来不说出你所要说的话。

Lest I should know you too easily, you play with me.

You blind me with flashes of laughter to hide your tears.

I know, I know your art,

You never say the word you would.

只恐我不珍爱你，你千方百计地闪避我。

只恐我把你和大家混在一起，你独自站在一边。

我知道，我知道你的妙计，

你从来不走你所要走的路。

Lest I should not prize you, you elude me in a thousand ways.

Lest I should confuse you with the crowd, you stand aside.

I know, I know your art,

You never walk the path you would.

你的要求比别人的都多，因此你才静默。

你用嬉笑的无心来回避我的赠与。

我知道，我知道你的妙计，

你从来不肯接受你想接受的东西。

Your claim is more than that of others, that is why you are silent.

With playful carelessness you avoid my gifts.

I know, I know your art,

You never will take what you would.

036

他低声说："我爱，抬起眼睛吧。"

我严厉地责骂他说："走！"但是他不动。

他站在我面前拉住我的双手。我说："躲开我！"但是他没有走。

He whispered, "My love, raise your eyes."

I sharply chid him, and said "Go!" But he did not stir.

He stood before me and held both my hands. I said, "Leave me!" But he did not go.

他把脸靠近我的耳边。我瞪他一眼说："不要脸！"但是他没有动。

他的嘴唇触到我的腮颊。我震颤了，说："你太大胆了！"但是他不怕丑。

He brought his face near my ear. I glanced at him and said, "What a shame!" But he did not move.

His lips touched my cheek. I trembled and said, "You dare too much." But he had no shame.

他把一朵花插在我发上。我说："这也没有用处！"但是他站着不动。

他取下我颈上的花环就走开了。我哭了，问我的心说："他为什么不回来呢？"

He put a flower in my hair. I said, "It is useless!" But he stood unmoved.

He took the garland from my neck and went away. I weep and ask my heart, "Why does he not come back?"

037

"你愿意把你的鲜花的花环挂在我的颈上么，佳人？"

"但是你要晓得，我编的那个花环，是为大家的，为那些偶然瞥见的人，住在未开发的大地上的人，住在诗人歌曲里的人。

Would you put your wreath of fresh flowers on my neck, fair one?

But you must know that the one wreath that I had woven is for the many, for those who are seen in glimpses, or dwell in lands unexplored, or live in poets'songs.

现在来请求我的心作为答赠已经太晚了。

曾有一个时候我的生命像一朵蓓蕾，它所有的芬芳都储藏在花心里。

现在它已经远远地喷溢四散。

谁晓得有什么魅力，可以把它们收集关闭起来呢？

我的心不容我只给一个人，它是要给与许多人的。"

It is too late to ask my heart in return for yours.

There was a time when my life was like a bud, all its perfume was stored in its core.

Now it is squandered far and wide.

Who knows the enchantment that can gather and shut it up again?

My heart is not mine to give to one only, it is given to the many.

038

我爱，从前有一天，你的诗人把一首伟大史诗投进他心里。

呵，我不小心，它打到你的叮当的脚镯上而引起悲愁。

它裂成诗歌的碎片散洒在你的脚边。

我满载的一切古代战争的货物，都被笑浪所颠簸，被眼泪浸透而下沉。

你必须使这损失成为我的收获，我爱。

如果我的死后不朽的荣名的要求都破灭了，那就在我生前使我不朽吧。

我将不为这损失伤心，也不责怪你。

My love, once upon a time your poet launched a great epic in his mind.

Alas, I was not careful, and it struck your ringing anklets and came to grief.

It broke up into scraps of songs and lay scattered at your feet.

All my cargo of the stories of old wars was tossed by the laughing waves and soaked in tears and sank.

You must make this loss good to me, my love.

If my claims to immortal fame after death are shattered, make me immortal while I live.

And I will not mourn for my loss nor blame you.

039

整个早晨我想编一个花环，但是花儿滑掉了。

你坐在一旁偷偷地从侦伺的眼角看着我。

问这一对沉黑的恶作剧的眼睛，这是谁的错。

I try to weave a wreath all the morning, but the flowers slip and they drop out.

You sit there watching me in secret through the corner of your prying eyes.

Ask those eyes, darkly planning mischief, whose fault it was.

我想唱一支歌，但是唱不出来。

一个暗笑在你唇上颤动；你问它我失败的缘由。

让你微笑的唇儿发一个誓，说我的歌声怎样地消失在沉默里，像一只在荷花里沉醉的蜜蜂。

I try to sing a song, but in vain.

A hidden smile trembles on your lips; ask of it the reason of my failure.

Let your smiling lips say on oath how my voice lost itself in silence like a drunken bee in the lotus.

夜晚了，是花瓣合起的时候了。

容许我坐在你的旁边，容许我的唇儿做那在沉默中、在星辰的微光中能做的工作吧。

It is evening, and the time for the flowers to close their petals.

Give me leave to sit by your side, and bid my lips to do the work that can be done in silence and in the dim light of stars.

040

一个怀疑的微笑在你眼中闪烁，当我来向你告别的时候。

我这样做的次数太多了，你想我很快又会回来。

告诉你实话，我自己心里也有同样的怀疑。

因为春天年年回来；满月道过别又来访问，花儿每年回来在枝上红晕着脸，很可能我向你告别只为的要再回到你的身边。

但是把这幻象保留一会吧，不要冷酷粗率地把它赶走。

当我说我要永远离开你的时候，就当作真话来接受它，让泪雾暂时加深你眼边的黑影。

当我再来的时候，随便你怎样地狡笑吧。

An unbelieving smile flits on your eyes when I come to you to take my leave.

I have done it so often that you think I will soon return.

To tell you the truth I have the same doubt in my mind.

For the spring days come again time after time; the full moon takes leave and comes on another visit, the flowers come again and blush upon their branches year after year, and it is likely that I take my leave only to come to you again.

But keep the illusion awhile; do not send it away with ungentle haste.

When I say I leave you for all time, accept it as true, and let a mist of tears for one moment deepen the dark rim of your eyes.

Then smile as archly as you like when I come again.

041

我想对你说出我要说的最深的话语，我不敢，我怕你哂笑。

因此我嘲笑自己，把我的秘密在玩笑中打碎。

我把我的痛苦说得轻松，因为怕你会这样做。

I long to speak the deepest words I have to say to you;
but I dare not, for fear you should laugh.

That is why I laugh at myself and shatter my secret in jest.

I make light of my pain, afraid you should do so.

我想对你说出我要说的最真的话语，我不敢，我怕你不信。

因此我弄真成假，说出和我的真心相反的话。

我把我的痛苦说得可笑，因为我怕你会这样做。

I long to tell you the truest words I have to say to you; but
I dare not, being afraid that you would not believe them.

That is why I disguise them in untruth, saying the contrary of what I mean.

I make my pain appear absurd, afraid that you should do so.

我想用最宝贵的名词来形容你，我不敢，我怕得不到相当的酬报。

因此我给你安上苛刻的名字，而夸示我的硬骨。

我伤害你，因为怕你永远不知道我的痛苦。

I long to use the most precious words I have for you; but I dare not, fearing I should not be paid with like value.

That is why I gave you hard names and boast of my callous strength.

I hurt you, for fear you should never know any pain.

我渴望静默地坐在你的身旁，我不敢，怕我的心会跳到我的唇上。

因此我轻松地说东道西，把我的心藏在语言的后面。

我粗暴地对待我的痛苦，因为我怕你会这样做。

I long to sit silent by you; but I dare not lest my heart
come out at my lips.

That is why I prattle and chatter lightly and hide my heart
behind words.

I rudely handle my pain, for fear you should do so.

我渴望从你身边走开，我不敢，怕你看出我的懦怯。

因此我随随便便地昂首走到你的面前。

从你眼里频频掷来的刺激，使我的痛苦永远新鲜。

I long to go away from your side; but I dare not, for fear
my cowardice should become known to you.

That is why I hold my head high and carelessly come into
your presence.

Constant thrusts from your eyes keep my pain fresh for
ever.

042

呵，疯狂的、头号的醉汉；

如果你踢开门户在大众面前装疯；

如果你在一夜倒空囊橐，对慎重轻蔑地弹着指头；

如果你走着奇怪的道路，和无益的东西游戏；

不理会韵律和理性；

如果你在风暴前扯起船帆，你把船舵折成两半，

那么我就要跟随你，伙伴，喝得烂醉走向堕落灭亡。

O mad, superbly drunk:

If you kick open your doors and play the fool in public;

If you empty your bag in a night, and snap your fingers
at prudence;

If you walk in curious paths and play with useless things;

Reck not rhyme or reason;

If unfurling your sails before the storm you snap the
rudder in two,

Then I will follow you, comrade, and be drunken and go
to the dogs.

我在稳重聪明的街坊中间虚度了日日夜夜。

过多的知识使我白了头发，过多的观察使我眼力模糊。

多年来我积攒了许多零碎的东西：

把这些东西摔碎，在上面跳舞，把它们散掷到风中去吧。

因为我知道喝得烂醉而堕落灭亡，是最高的智慧。

I have wasted my days and nights in the company of steady wise neighbours.

Much knowing has turned my hair grey, and much watching has made my sight dim.

For years I have gathered and heaped up scraps and fragments of things:

Crush them and dance upon them, and scatter them all to the winds.

For I know it is the height of wisdom to be drunken and go to the dogs.

让一切歪曲的顾虑消亡吧，让我无望地迷失了路途。

让一阵旋风吹来，把我连船锚一齐卷走。

世界上住着高尚的人，劳动的人，有用又聪明。

有的人很从容地走在前头，有的人庄重地走在后面。

让他们快乐繁荣吧，让我傻呆地无用吧。

因为我知道喝得烂醉而堕落灭亡，是一切工作的结局。

Let all crooked scruples vanish, let me hopelessly lose my way.

Let a gust of wild giddiness come and sweep me away from my anchors.

The world is peopled with worthies, and workers, useful and clever.

There are men who are easily first, and men who come decently after.

Let them be happy and prosper, and let me be foolishly futile.

For I know it is the end of all works to be drunken and go to the dogs.

我此刻誓将一切的要求，让给正人君子。

我抛弃我学识的自豪和是非的判断。

我打碎记忆的瓶壶，挥洒最后的眼泪。

以红果酒的泡沫来洗澡，使我欢笑发出光辉。

我暂且撕裂温恭和认真的标志。

我将发誓作一个无用的人，喝得烂醉而堕落灭亡下去。

I swear to surrender this moment all claims to the ranks of the decent.

I let go my pride of learning and judgment of right and of wrong.

I'll shatter memory's vessel, scattering the last drop of tears.

With the foam of the berry-red wine I will bathe and brighten my laughter.

The badge of the civil and staid I'll tear into shreds for the nonce.

I'll take the holy vow to be worthless, to be drunken and go to the dogs.

043

不，我的朋友，我永不会做一个苦行者，随便你怎么说。

我将永不做一个苦行者，假如她不和我一同受戒。

这是我坚定的决心，如果我找不到一个阴凉的住处和一个忏悔的伴侣，我将永远不会变成一个苦行者。

No, my friends, I shall never be an ascetic, whatever you may say.

I shall never be an ascetic if she does not take the vow with me.

It is my firm resolve that if I cannot find a shady shelter and a companion for my penance, I shall never turn ascetic.

不，我的朋友，我将永不离开我的炉火与家庭，去退隐到深林里面，

如果在林荫中没有欢笑的回响；如果没有郁金色的衣裙在风

中飘扬；

如果它的幽静不因有轻柔的微语而加深。

我将永不会做一个苦行者。

No, my friends, I shall never leave my hearth and home, and retire into the forest solitude, if rings no merry laughter in its echoing shade and if the end of no saffron mantle flutters in the wind; if its silence is not deepened by soft whispers.

I shall never be an ascetic.

044

尊敬的长者，饶恕这一对罪人吧。

今天春风猖狂地吹起旋舞，把尘土和枯叶都扫走了，你的功课也随着一起丢掉了。

师父，不要说生命是虚空的。

因为我们和死亡订下一次和约，在一段温馨的时间中，我俩变成不朽。

Reverend sir, forgive this pair of sinners. Spring winds today are blowing in wild eddies, driving dust and dead leaves away, and with them your lessons are all lost.

Do not say, father, that life is a vanity.

For we have made truce with death for once, and only for a few fragrant hours we two have been made immortal.

即使是国王的军队凶猛地前来追捕，我们将忧愁地摇头说，弟兄们，你们搅扰了我们了。如果你们必须做这个吵闹的游戏，到别处去敲击你们的武器吧。因为我们刚在这片刻飞逝的时光中变成不朽。

Even if the king's army came and fiercely fell upon us we should sadly shake our heads and say, "Brothers, you are disturbing us. If you must have this noisy game, go and clatter your arms elsewhere. Since only for a few fleeting moments we have been made immortal."

如果亲切的人们来把我们围起，我们将恭敬地向他们鞠躬说，这个荣幸使我们惭愧。在我们居住的无限天空之中，没有多少隙地。因为在春天繁花盛开，蜜蜂的忙碌的翅翼也彼此摩挤。只住着我们两个仙人的小天堂，是狭小得太可笑了。

If friendly people came and flocked around us, we should humbly bow to them and say, "This extravagant good fortune is an embarrassment to us. Room is scarce in the infinite sky where we dwell. For in the springtime flowers come in crowds, and the busy wings of bees jostle each other. Our little heaven, where dwell only we two immortals, is too absurdly narrow."

045

对那些定要离开的客人们，求神帮他们快走，并且扫掉他们所有的足迹。

把舒服的单纯的亲近的，微笑着一起抱在你的怀里。

今天是幻影的节日，他们不知道自己的死期。

让你的笑声只作为无意义的欢乐，像浪花上的闪光。

让你的生命像露珠的叶尖一样，在时间的边缘上轻轻跳舞。

在你的琴弦上弹出无定的暂时的音调吧。

To the guests that must go bid God'speed and brush away all traces of their steps.

Take to your bosom with a smile what is easy and simple and near.

To-day is the festival of phantoms that know not when they die.

Let your laughter be but a meaningless mirth like twinkles of light on the ripples.

Let your life lightly dance on the edges of Time like dew on the tip of a leaf.

Strike in chords from your harp fitful momentary rhythms.

046

你离开我自己走了。

我想我将为你忧伤，还将用金色的诗歌铸成你孤寂的形象，供养在我的心里。

但是，我的运气多坏，时间是短促的。

You left me and went on your way.

I thought I should mourn for you and set your solitary image in my heart wrought in a golden song.

But ah, my evil fortune, time is short.

青春一年一年地消逝；春日是暂时的；柔弱的花朵无意义地凋谢，聪明人警告我说，生命只是一颗荷叶上的露珠。

我可以不管这些，只凝望着背弃我的那个人么？

这会是无益的，愚蠢的，因为时间是太短暂了。

Youth wanes year after year; the spring days are fugitive; the frail flowers die for nothing, and the wise man warns me that life is but a dewdrop on the lotus leaf.

Should I neglect all this to gaze after one who has turned her back on me?

That would be rude and foolish, for time is short.

那么，来吧，我的雨夜的脚步声；微笑吧，我的金色的秋天；来吧，无虑无忧的四月，散掷着你的亲吻。

你来吧，还有你，也有你！

我的情人们，你知道我们都是凡人。为一个取回她的心的人而心碎，是件聪明的事情么？因为时间是短暂的。

Then, come, my rainy nights with pattering feet; smile, my golden autumn; come, careless April, scattering your kisses abroad.

You come, and you, and you also!

My loves, you know we are mortals. Is it wise to break one's heart for the one who takes her heart away? For time is short.

坐在屋角凝思，把我的世界中的你们都写在韵律里，是甜柔的。

把自己的忧伤抱紧，决不受人安慰，是英勇的。

但是一个新的面庞，在我门外偷窥，抬起眼来看我的眼睛。

我只能拭去眼泪，更改我歌曲的腔调。

因为时间是短暂的。

It is sweet to sit in a corner to muse and write in rhymes that you are all my world.

It is heroic to hug one's sorrow and determine not to be consoled.

But a fresh face peeps across my door and raises its eyes to my eyes.

I cannot but wipe away my tears and change the tune of my song.

For time is short.

047

如果你要这样，我就停了歌唱。

如果它使你心震颤，我就把眼光从你脸上挪开。

如果使你在行走时忽然惊跃，我就躲开另走别路。

如果在你编串花环时，使你烦乱，我就避开你寂寞的花园。

如果我使水花飞溅，我就不在你的河边划船。

If you would have it so, I will end my singing.

If it sets your heart aflutter, I will take away my eyes from
your face.

If it suddenly startles you in your walk, I will step aside
and take another path.

If it confuses you in your flower-weaving, I will shun your
lonely garden.

If it makes the water wanton and wild, I will not row my
boat by your bank.

048

　　把我从你甜柔的枷束中放出来吧，我爱，不要再斟上亲吻的酒。

　　香烟的浓雾窒塞了我的心。

　　开起门来，让晨光进入吧！

　　我消失在你里面，包缠在你爱抚的折痕之中。

　　把我从你的诱惑中放出来吧，把男子气概交还我，好让我把得到自由的心贡献给你。

Free me from the bonds of your sweetness, my love! No more of this wine of kisses.

This mist of heavy incense stifles my heart.

Open the doors, make room for the morning light.

I am lost in you, wrapped in the folds of your caresses.

Free me from your spells, and give me back the manhood to offer you my freed heart.

049

我握住她的手把她抱紧在胸前。

我想以她的爱娇来填满我的怀抱，用亲吻来偷劫她的甜笑，用我的眼睛来吸饮她的深黑的一瞥。

呵，但是，它在哪里呢？谁能从天空滤出蔚蓝呢？

我想去把握美；它躲开我，只有躯体留在我的手里。

失望而困乏地，我回来了。

躯体哪能触到那只有精神才能触到的花朵呢？

I hold her hands and press her to my breast.

I try to fill my arms with her loveliness, to plunder her sweet smile with kisses, to drink her dark glances with my eyes.

Ah, but, where is it? Who can strain the blue from the sky?

I try to grasp the beauty; it eludes me, leaving only the body in my hands.

Baffled and weary I come back.

How can the body touch the flower which only the spirit may touch?

050

爱，我的心日夜想望和你相见——那像吞灭一切的死亡一样的会见。

像一阵风暴把我卷走；把我的一切都拿去；劈开我的睡眠抢走我的梦。剥夺了我的世界。

在这毁灭里，在精神的全部赤露里，让我们在美中合一吧。

我的空想是可怜的！除了在你里面，哪有这合一的希望呢，我的神?

Love, my heart longs day and night for meeting with you—for the meeting that is like all-devouring death.

Sweep me away like a storm; take everything I have; break open my sleep and plunder my dreams. Rob me of my world.

In that devastation, in the utter nakedness of spirit, let us become one in beauty.

Alas for my vain desire! Where is this hope for union except in thee, my God?

051

那么唱完最后一支歌就让我们走吧。

当这夜过完就把这夜忘掉。

我想把谁紧抱在臂里呢？梦是永不会被捉住的。

我渴望的双手把"空虚"紧压在我心上，压碎了我的胸膛。

Then finish the last song and let us leave.

Forget this night when the night is no more.

Whom do I try clasp in my arms? Dreams can never be made captive.

My eager hands press emptiness to my heart and it bruises my breast.

052

灯为什么熄了呢?

我用斗篷遮住它怕它被风吹灭，因此灯熄了。

Why did the lamp go out?

I shaded it with my cloak to save it from the wind, that is why the lamp went out.

花为什么谢了呢?

我的热恋的爱把它紧压在我的心上，因此花谢了。

Why did the flower fade?

I pressed it to my heart with anxious love, that is why the flower faded.

泉为什么干了呢?

我盖起一道堤把它拦起给我使用，因此泉干了。

Why did the stream dry up?

I put a dam across it to have it for my use, that is why the stream dried up.

琴弦为什么断了呢?

我强弹一个它力不能胜的音节，因此琴弦断了。

Why did the harp-string break?

I tried to force a note that was beyond its power, that is why the harp-string is broken.

053

为什么盯着我使我羞愧呢？

我不是来求乞的。

只为要消磨时光，我才来站在你院边的篱外。

为什么盯着我使我羞愧呢？

Why do you put me to shame with a look?

I have not come as a beggar.

Only for a passing hour I stood at the end of your courtyard outside the garden hedge.

Why do you put me to shame with a look?

我没有从你园里采走一朵玫瑰，没有摘下一颗果子。

我谦卑地在任何生客都可站立的路边棚下，找个荫蔽。

我没有采走一朵玫瑰。

Not a rose did I gather from your garden, not a fruit did I pluck.

I humbly took my shelter under the wayside shade where every strange traveller may stand.

Not a rose did I pluck.

是的，我的脚疲乏了，骤雨又落了下来。

风在摇曳的竹林中呼叫。

云阵像败退似的跑过天空。

我的脚疲乏了。

Yes, my feet were tired, and the shower of rain came down.

The winds cried out among the swaying bamboo branches.

The clouds ran across the sky as though in the flight from defeat.

My feet were tired.

我不知道你怎样看待我，或是你在门口等什么人。

闪电昏眩了你看望的目光。

我怎能知道你会看到站在黑暗中的我呢?

我不知道你怎样看待我。

I know not what you thought of me or for whom you were waiting at your door.

Flashes of lightning dazzled your watching eyes.

How could I know that you could see me where I stood in the dark?

I know not what you thought of me.

白日过尽,雨势暂停。

我离开你园畔的树荫和草地上的座位。

日光已暗;关上你的门户吧;我走我的路。

白日过尽了。

The day is ended, and the rain has ceased for a moment.

I leave the shadow of the tree at the end of your garden and this seat on the grass.

It has darkened; shut your door; I go my way.

The day is ended.

054

市集已过，你在夜晚急急地提着篮子要到哪里去呢？

他们都挑着担子回家去了；月亮从村树隙中下窥。

唤船的回声从深黑的水上传到远处野鸭睡眠的沼泽。

在市集已过的时候，你提着篮子急忙地要到哪里去呢？

Where do you hurry with your basket this late evening when the marketing is over?

They all have come home with their burdens; the moon peeps from above the village trees.

The echoes of the voices calling for the ferry run across the dark water to the distant swamp where wild ducks sleep.

Where do you hurry with your basket when the marketing is over?

睡眠把她的手指按在大地的双眼上。

鸦巢已静，竹叶的微语也已沉默。

劳动的人们从田间归来，把席子展铺在院子里。

在市集已过的时候，你提着篮子急忙地要到哪里去呢？

Sleep has laid her fingers upon the eyes of the earth.

The nests of the crows have become silent, and the murmurs of the bamboo leaves are silent.

The labourers home from their fields spread their mats in the courtyards.

Where do you hurry with your basket when the marketing is over?

055

正午的时候你走了。

烈日当空。

当你走的时候，我已做完了工作，坐在凉台上。

It was midday when you went away.

The sun was strong in the sky.

I had done my work and sat alone on my balcony when you went away.

不定的风吹来，含带着许多远野的香气。

鸽子在树荫中不停地叫唤，一只蜜蜂在我屋里飞着，嗡出许多远野的消息。

Fitful gusts came winnowing through the smells of many distant fields.

The doves cooed tireless in the shade, and a bee strayed in my room humming the news of many distant fields.

村庄在午热中入睡了。路上无人。

树叶的声音时起时息。

我凝望天空，把一个我知道的人的名字织在蔚蓝里，当村庄在午热中入睡的时候。

The village slept in the noonday heat. The road lay deserted.

In sudden fits the rustling of the leaves rose and died.

I glazed at the sky and wove in the blue the letters of a name I had known, while the village slept in the noonday heat.

我忘记把头发编起。困倦的风在我颊上和它嬉戏。

河水在荫岸下平静地流着。

懒散的白云动也不动。

我忘了编起我的头发。

I had forgotten to braid my hair. The languid breeze played with it upon my cheek.

The river ran unruffled under the shady bank.

The lazy white clouds did not move.

I had forgotten to braid my hair.

正午的时候你走了。

路上尘土灼热，田野在喘息。

鸽子在密叶中呼唤。

我独坐在凉台上，当你走的时候。

It was midday when you went away.

The dust of the road was hot and the fields panting.

The doves cooed among the dense leaves.

I was alone in my balcony when you went away.

056

我是妇女中为平庸的日常家务而忙碌的一个。

你为什么把我挑选出来，把我从日常生活的凉荫中带出来？

I was one among many women busy with the obscure daily tasks of the household.

Why did you single me out and bring me away from the cool shelter of our common life?

没有表现出来的爱是神圣的。它像宝石般在隐藏的心的朦胧里放光。在奇异的日光中，它显得可怜地晦暗。

呵，你打碎我心的盖子，把我颤栗的爱情拖到空旷的地方，把那阴暗的藏我心巢的一角，永远破坏了。

Love unexpressed is sacred. It shines like gems in the gloom of the hidden heart. In the light of the curious day it looks pitifully dark.

Ah, you broke through the cover of my heart and dragged my trembling love into the open place, destroying for ever the shady corner where it hid its nest.

　　别的女人和从前一样。

　　没有一个人窥探到自己的最深处，她们不知道自己的秘密。

　　她们轻快地微笑，哭泣，谈话，工作。她们每天到庙里去，点上她们的灯，还到河中取水。

The other women are the same as ever.

No one has peeped into their inmost being, and they themselves know not their own secret.

Lightly they smile, and weep, chatter, and work. Daily they go to the temple, light their lamps, and fetch water from the river.

　　我希望能从无遮拦的颤羞中把我的爱情救出，但是你掉头不顾。

是的，你的前途是远大的，但是你把我的归路切断了，让我在世界的无睫毛的眼睛日夜瞪视之下赤裸着。

I hoped my love would be saved from the shivering shame of the shelterless, but you turn your face away.

Yes, your path lies open before you, but you have cut off my return, and left me stripped naked before the world with its lidless eyes staring night and day.

057

我采了你的花，呵，世界！

我把它压在胸前，花刺伤了我。

日光渐暗，我发现花儿凋谢了，痛苦却存留着。

I plucked your flower, O world!

I pressed it to my heart and the thorn pricked.

When the day waned and it darkened, I found that the flower had faded, but the pain remained.

许多有香有色的花又将来到你这里，呵，世界。

但是我采花的时代过去了，黑夜悠悠，我没有了玫瑰，只有痛苦存留着。

More flowers will come to you with perfume and pride, O world!

But my time for flower-gathering is over, and
through the dark night I have not my rose, only the pain
remains.

058

有一天早晨，一个盲女来献给我一串盖在荷叶下的花环。

我把它挂在颈上，泪水涌上我的眼睛。

我吻了她，说："你和花朵一样地盲目。

"你自己不知道你的礼物是多么美丽。"

One morning in the flower garden a blind girl came to offer me a flower-chain in the cover of a lotus leaf.

I put it round my neck, and tears came to my eyes.

I kissed her and said, "You are blind even as the flowers are.

"You yourself know not how beautiful is your gift."

059

呵，女人，你不但是神的，而且是人的手工艺品；他们永远从心里用美来打扮你。

诗人们用比喻的金线替你织网，画家们给你的身形以永新的不朽。

海献上珍珠，矿献上金子，夏日的花园献上花朵来装扮你，覆盖你，使你更加美妙。

人类心中的愿望，在你的青春上洒上光荣。

你一半是女人，一半是梦。

O woman, you are not merely the handiwork of God, but also of men; these are ever endowing you with beauty from their hearts.

Poets are weaving for you a web with threads of golden imagery; painters are giving your form ever new immortality.

The sea gives its pearls, the mines their gold, the summer gardens their flowers to deck you, to cover you, to make you more precious.

The desire of men's hearts has shed its glory over your youth.

You are one-half woman and one-half dream.

the feather that she is only over your...

You are one.... woman and longs it dream...

060

在生命奔腾怒吼的中流，呵，石头雕成的"美"，你冷静无言，独自超绝地站立着。

"伟大的时间"依恋地坐在你脚边低语说：

"说话吧，对我说话吧，我爱，说话吧，我的新娘！"

但是你的话被石头关住了，呵，"不动的美"！

Amidst the rush and roar of life, O Beauty, carved in stone, you stand mute and still, alone and aloof.

Great Time sits enamoured at your feet and murmurs:

"Speak, speak to me, my love; speak, my bride!"

But your speech is shut up in stone, O Immovable Beauty!

061

安静吧，我的心，让别离的时间甜柔吧。

让它不是个死亡而是圆满。

让爱恋融入记忆，痛苦融入诗歌吧。

让穿越天空的飞翔在巢上敛翼中终止。

让你双手的最后的接触，像夜中花朵一样地温柔。

站住一会吧，呵，"美丽的结局"，用沉默说出最后的话语吧。

我向你鞠躬，举起我的灯来照亮你的归途。

Peace, my heart, let the time for the parting be sweet.

Let it not be a death but completeness.

Let love melt into memory and pain into songs.

Let the flight through the sky end in the folding of the wings over the nest.

Let the last touch of your hands be gentle like the flower of the night.

Stand still, O Beautiful End, for a moment, and say your

last words in silence.

I bow to you and hold up my lamp to light you on your way.

062

在梦境的朦胧小路上，我去寻找我前生的爱。

In the dusky path of a dream I went to seek the love who was mine in a former life.

她的房子是在冷静的街尾。

在晚风中，她爱养的孔雀在架上昏睡，鸽子在自己的角落里沉默着。

Her house stood at the end of a desolate street.

In the evening breeze her pet peacock sat drowsing on its perch, and the pigeons were silent in their corner.

她把灯放在门边，站在我面前。

她抬起一双大眼望着我的脸，无言地问道："你好么，我的朋友？"

我想回答，但是我们的语言迷失而又忘却了。

She set her lamp down by the portal and stood before me.

She raised her large eyes to my face and mutely asked, "Are you well, my friend?"

I tried to answer, but our language had been lost and forgotten.

我想来想去，怎么也想不起我们叫什么名字。

眼泪在她眼中闪光，她向我伸出右手。我握住她的手静默地站着。

I thought and thought; our names would not come to my mind.

Tears shone in her eyes. She held up her right hand to me. I took it and stood silent.

我们的灯在晚风中颤摇着熄灭了。

Our lamp had flickered in the evening breeze and
died.

063

行路人，你必须走么？

夜是静寂的，黑暗在树林上昏睡。

我们的凉台上灯火辉煌，繁花鲜美，青春的眼睛还清醒着。

你离开的时间到了么？

行路人，你必须走么？

Traveller, must you go?

The night is still and the darkness swoons upon the forest.

The lamps are bright in our balcony, the flowers all fresh,
and the youthful eyes still awake.

Is the time for your parting come?

Traveller, must you go?

我们不曾用恳求的手臂来抱住你的双足。

你的门开着。你的立在门外的马，也已上了鞍鞯。

如果我们想拦住你的去路，也只是用我们的歌曲。

如果我们曾想挽留你，也只是用我们的眼睛。

行路人，我们没有希望留住你，我们只有眼泪。

We have not bound your feet with our entreating arms.

Your doors are open. Your horse stands saddled at the gate.

If we have tried to bar your passage it was but with our songs.

Did we ever try to hold you back it was but with our eyes.

Traveller, we are helpless to keep you. We have only our tears.

在你眼里发光的是什么样的不灭之火?

在你血管中奔流的是什么样的不宁的热力?

从黑暗中有什么召唤在引动你?

What quenchless fire glows in your eyes?

What restless fever runs in your blood?

What call from the dark urges you?

你从天上的星星中，念到什么可怕的咒语，就是黑夜沉默而异样地走进你心中时带来的那个密封的秘密的消息？

如果你不喜欢那热闹的集会，如果你需要安静，困乏的心呵，我们就吹灭灯火，停止琴声。

我们将在风叶声中静坐在黑暗里，倦乏的月亮将在你窗上洒上苍白的光辉。

呵，行路人，是什么不眠的精灵从中夜的心中和你接触了呢？

What awful incantation have you read among the stars in the sky, that with a sealed secret message the night entered your heart, silent and strange?

If you do not care for merry meetings, if you must have peace, weary heart, we shall put our lamps out and silence our harps.

We shall sit still in the dark in the rustle of leaves, and the tired moon will shed pale rays on your window.

O traveller, what sleepless spirit has touched you from the heart of the mid-night?

064

我在大路灼热的尘土上消磨了一天。

现在，在晚凉中我敲着一座小庙的门。这庙已经荒废倒塌了。

一棵愁苦的菩提树，从破墙的裂缝里伸展出饥饿的爪根。

I spent my day on the scorching hot dust of the road.

Now, in the cool of the evening, I knock at the door of the inn. It is deserted and in ruins.

A grim ashath tree spreads its hungry clutching roots through the gaping fissures of the walls.

从前曾有过路人到这里来洗疲乏的脚。

他们在新月的微光中在院里摊开席子，坐着谈论异地的风光。

早起他们精神恢复了，鸟声使他们欢悦，友爱的花儿在道边向他们点首。

Days have been when wayfarers came here to wash their weary feet.

They spread their mats in the courtyard in the dim light of the early moon, and sat and talked of strange lands.

They work refreshed in the morning when birds made them glad, and friendly flowers nodded their heads at them from the wayside.

但是当我来的时候没有灯在等待我。

只有残留的灯烟熏污的黑迹，像盲人的眼睛，从墙上瞪视着我。

萤虫在涸池边的草里闪烁，竹影在荒芜的小径上摇曳。

我在一天之末做了没有主人的客人。

在我面前的是漫漫的长夜，我疲倦了。

But no lighted lamp awaited me when I came here.

The black smudges of smoke left by many a forgotten evening lamp stare, like blind eyes, from the wall.

Fireflies flit in the bush near the dried-up pond, and bamboo branches fling their shadows on the grass-grown path.

I am the guest of no one at the end of my day.

The long night is before me, and I am tired.

065

又是你呼唤我么？

夜来到了，困乏像爱的恳求用双臂围抱住我。

你叫我了么？

Is that your call again?

The evening has come. Weariness clings around me like the arms of entreating love.

Do you call me?

我已把整天的工夫给了你，残忍的主妇，你还定要掠夺我的夜晚么？

万事都有个终结，黑暗的静寂是个人独有的。

你的声音定要穿透黑暗来刺击我么？

I had given all my day to you, cruel mistress, must you

also rob me of my night?

Somewhere there is an end to everything, and the loneness of the dark is one's own.

Must your voice cut through it and smite me?

难道你门前的夜晚没有音乐和睡眠么?

难道那翅翼不响的星辰,从来不攀登你的不仁之塔的上空么?

难道你园中的花朵,永不在绵软的死亡中堕地么?

Has the evening no music of sleep at your gate?

Do the silent-winged stars never climb the sky above your pitiless tower?

Do the flowers never drop on the dust in soft death in your garden?

你定要叫我么,你这不安静的人?

那就让爱的愁眼,徒然地因着盼望而流泪。

让灯盏在空屋里点着。

让渡船载那些困乏的工人回家。

我把梦想丢下，来奔赴你的召唤。

Must you call me, you unquiet one?

Then let the sad eyes of love vainly watch and weep.

Let the lamp burn in the lonely house.

Let the ferry-boat take the weary labourers to their home.

I leave behind my dreams and I hasten to your call.

066

一个流浪的疯子在寻找点金石，他褐黄的头发乱蓬蓬地蒙着尘土，身体瘦得像个影子，他双唇紧闭，就像他的紧闭的心门。他的烧红的眼睛就像萤火虫的灯亮在寻找他的爱侣。

A wandering madman was seeking the touchstone, with matted locks, tawny and dust-laden, and body worn to a shadow, his lips tight-pressed, like the shut-up doors of his heart, his burning eyes like the lamp of a glow-worm seeking its mate.

无边的海在他面前怒吼。

喧哗的波浪，在不停地谈论那隐藏的珠宝，嘲笑那不懂得它们的意思的愚人。

也许现在他不再有希望了，但是他不肯休息，因为寻求变成他的生命——

就像海洋永远向天伸臂要求不可得到的东西——

就像星辰绕着圈走，却要寻找一个永不能到达的目标——

在那寂寞的海边，那头发垢乱的疯子，也仍旧徘徊着寻找点金石。

Before him the endless ocean roared.

The garrulous waves ceaselessly talked of hidden treasures, mocking the ignorance that knew not their meaning.

Maybe he now had no hope remaining, yet he would not rest, for the search had become his life—

Just as the ocean for ever lifts its arms to the sky for the unattainable—

Just as the stars go in circles, yet seeking a goal that can never be reached—

Even so on the lonely shore the madman with dusty tawny locks still roamed in search of the touchstone.

有一天，一个村童走上来问："告诉我，你腰上的那条金链是从哪里来的呢？"

疯子吓了一跳——那条本来是铁的链子真的变成金的了；这不

是一场梦，但是他不知道是什么时候变了的。

他狂乱地敲着自己的前额——什么时候，呵，什么时候在他的不知不觉之中得到成功了呢？

拾起大石去碰碰那条链子，然后不看看变化与否，又把它扔掉，这已成了习惯；就是这样，这疯子找到了又失掉了那块点金石。

One day a village boy came up and asked, "Tell me, where did you come at this golden chain about your waist?"

The madman started—the chain that once was iron was verily gold; it was not a dream, but he did not know when it had changed.

He struck his forehead wildly—where, O where had he without knowing it achieved success?

It had grown into a habit, to pick up pebbles and touch the chain, and to throw them away without looking to see if a change had come; thus the madman found and lost the touchstone.

太阳沉西，天空灿金。

疯子沿着自己的脚印走回，去寻找他失去的珍宝。他气力尽消，身体弯曲，他的心像连根拔起的树一样，萎垂在尘土里了。

The sun was sinking low in the west, the sky was of gold.

The madman returned on his footsteps to seek anew the lost treasure, with his strength gone, his body bent, and his heart in the dust, like a tree uprooted.

067

虽然夜晚缓步走来，让一切歌声停息；

虽然你的伙伴都去休息而你也倦乏了；

虽然恐怖在黑暗中弥漫，天空的脸也被面纱遮起；

但是，鸟儿，我的鸟儿，听我的话，不要垂翅吧。

Though the evening comes with slow steps and has signalled for all songs to cease;

Though your companions have gone to their rest and you are tired;

Though fear broods in the dark and the face of the sky is veiled;

Yet, bird, O my bird, listen to me, do not close your wings.

这不是林中树叶的阴影，这是大海涨溢，像一条深黑的龙蛇。

这不是盛开的茉莉花的跳舞，这是闪光的水沫。

呵，何处是阳光下的绿岸，何处是你的窝巢？

鸟儿，呵，我的鸟儿，听我的话，不要垂翅吧。

That is not the gloom of the leaves of the forest, that is the sea swelling like a dark black snake.

That is not the dance of the flowering jasmine, that is flashing foam.

Ah, where is the sunny green shore, where is your nest?

Bird, O my bird, listen to me, do not close your wings.

长夜躺在你的路边，黎明在朦胧的山后睡眠。

星辰屏息地数着时间，柔弱的月儿在夜中浮泛。

鸟儿，呵，我的鸟儿，听我的话，不要垂翅吧。

The lone night lies along your path, the dawn sleeps behind the shadowy hills.

The stars hold their breath counting the hours, the feeble moon swims the deep night.

Bird, O my bird, listen to me, do not close your wings.

对于你，这里没有希望，没有恐怖。

这里没有消息，没有低语，没有呼唤。

这里没有家，没有休息的床。

这里只有你自己的一双翅翼和无路的天空。

鸟儿，呵，我的鸟儿，听我的话，不要垂翅吧。

There is no hope, no fear for you.

There is no word, no whisper, no cry.

There is no home, no bed for rest.

There is only your own pair of wings and the pathless sky.

Bird, O my bird, listen to me, do not close your wings.

068

没有人永远活着，弟兄，没有东西能以经久。把这紧记在心及时行乐吧。

我们的生命不是那个旧的负担，我们的道路不是那条长的旅程。

一个单独的诗人，不必去唱一支旧歌。

花儿萎谢；但是戴花的人不必永远悲伤。

弟兄，把这个紧记在心及时行乐吧。

None lives for ever, brother, and nothing lasts for long. Keep that in mind and rejoice.

Our life is not the one old burden, our path is not the one long journey.

One sole poet has not to sing one aged song.

The flower fades and dies; but he who wears the flower has not to mourn for it for ever.

Brother, keep that in mind and rejoice.

必须有一段完全的停歇，好把"圆满"编进音乐。

生命向它的黄昏下落，为了沉浸于金影之中。

必须从游戏中把"爱"召回，去饮忧伤之酒，再去生于泪天。

弟兄，把这紧记在心及时行乐吧。

There must come a full pause to weave perfection into music.

Life droops toward its sunset to be drowned in the golden shadows.

Love must be called from its play to drink sorrow and be borne to the heaven of tears.

Brother, keep that in mind and rejoice.

我们忙去采花，怕被过路的风偷走。

去夺取稍纵即逝的接吻，使我们血液奔流双目发光。

我们的生命是热切的，愿望是强烈的，因为时间在敲着离别之钟。

弟兄，把这紧记在心及时行乐吧。

We hasten to gather our flowers lest they are plundered by the passing winds.

It quickens our blood and brightens our eyes to snatch kisses that would vanish if we delayed.

Our life is eager, our desires are keen, for time tolls the bell of parting.

Brother, keep that in mind and rejoice.

我们没有时间去把握一件事物，揉碎它又把它丢在地上。

时间急速地走过。把梦幻藏在裙底。

我们的生命是短促的；只有几天恋爱的工夫。

若是为工作和劳役，生命就变得无尽的漫长。

弟兄，把这紧记在心及时行乐吧。

There is not time for us to clasp a thing and crush it and fling it away to the dust.

The hours trip rapidly away, hiding their dreams in their skirts.

Our life is short; it yields but a few days for love.

Were it for work and drudgery it would be endlessly long.

Brother, keep that in mind and rejoice.

美对我们是甜柔的，因为她和我们生命的快速调子应节舞蹈。

知识对我们是宝贵的，因为我们永不会有时间去完成它。

一切都在永生的天上做完。但是大地的幻象的花朵，却被死亡保持得永远新鲜。

弟兄，把这紧记在心及时行乐吧。

Beauty is sweet to us, because she dances to the same fleeting tune with our lives.

Knowledge is precious to us, because we shall never have time to complete it.

All is done and finished in the eternal Heaven. But earth's flowers of illusion are kept eternally fresh by death.

Brother, keep that in mind and rejoice.

069

我要追逐金鹿。

你也许会讪笑，我的朋友，但是我追求那逃避我的幻象。

我翻山越谷，我游遍许多无名的土地，因为我要追逐金鹿。

你到市场采买，满载着回家，但不知从何时何地一阵无家之风吹到我身上。

我心中无牵无挂；我把一切所有都撇在后面。

我翻山越谷，我游遍许多无名的土地——因为我在追逐金鹿。

I hunt for the golden stag.

You may smile, my friends, but I pursue the vision that eludes me.

I run across hills and dales, I wander through nameless lands, because I am hunting for the golden stag.

You come and buy in the market and go back to your homes laden with goods, but the spell of the homeless winds has touched me I know not when and where.

I have no care in my heart; all my belongings I have left

far behind me.

I run across hills and dales, I wander through nameless lands—because I am hunting for the golden stag.

070

我记得在童年时代，有一天我在水沟里漂一只纸船。

那是七月的一个阴湿的天，我独自快乐地嬉戏。

我在沟里漂一只纸船。

I remember a day in my childhood I floated a paper boat in the ditch.

It was a wet day of July; I was alone and happy over my play.

I floated my paper boat in the ditch.

忽然间阴云密布，狂风怒号，大雨倾注。

浑水像小河般流溢，把我的船冲没了。

我心里难过地想，这风暴是故意来破坏我的快乐的；它的一切恶意都是对着我的。

Suddenly the storm clouds thickened, winds came in gusts, and rain poured in torrents.

Rills of muddy water rushed and swelled the stream and sunk my boat.

Bitterly I thought in my mind that the storm came on purpose to spoil my happiness; all its malice was against me.

今天，七月的阴天是漫长的，我在默忆我生命中以我为失败者的一切游戏。

我抱怨命运，因为它屡次戏弄了我，当我忽然忆起我的沉在沟里的纸船的时候。

The cloudy day of July is long today, and I have been musing over all those games in life wherein I was loser.

I was blaming my fate for the many tricks it played on me, when suddenly I remembered the paper boat that sank in the ditch.

071

白日未尽，河岸上的市集未散。

我只恐我的时间浪掷了，我的最后一文钱也丢掉了。

但是，没有，我的兄弟，我还有些剩余。命运并没有把我的一切都骗走。

The day is not yet done, the fair is not over, the fair on the river-bank.

I had feared that my time had been squandered and my last penny lost.

But no, my brother. I have still something left. My fate has not cheated me of everything.

买卖做完了。

两边的手续费都收过了，该是我回家的时候了。

但是，看门的，你要你的辛苦钱么？

别怕，我还有点剩余。命运并没有把我的一切都骗走。

The selling and buying are over.

All the dues on both sides have been gathered in, and it is time for me to go home.

But, gatekeeper, do you ask for your toll?

Do not fear, I have still something left. My fate has not cheated me of everything.

风声宣布着风暴的威胁，西方低垂的云影预报着恶兆。

静默的河水在等候着狂风。

我怕被黑夜赶上，急忙过河。

The lull in the wind threatens storm, and the lowering clouds in the west bode no good.

The hushed water waits for the wind.

I hurry to cross the river before the night overtakes me.

呵，船夫，你要收费!

是的，兄弟，我还有些剩余。命运并没有把我的一切都骗走。

O ferryman, you want your fee!

Yes, brother, I have still something left. My fate has not
cheated me of everything.

路边树下坐着一个乞丐。可怜呵，他含着羞怯的希望看着我
的脸！

他以为我富足地携带着一天的利润。

是的，兄弟，我还有点剩余。命运并没有把我的一切都骗走。

In the wayside under the tree sits the beggar. Alas, he
looks at my face with a timid hope!

He thinks I am rich with the day's profit.

Yes, brother, I have still something left. My fate has not
cheated me of everything.

夜色愈深，路上静寂。萤火在草间闪烁。

谁以悄悄的蹑步在跟着我？

呵，我知道，你想掠夺我的一切获得。我必不使你失望！

因为我还有些剩余。命运并没有把我的一切都骗走。

The night grows dark and the road lonely. Fireflies gleam among the leaves.

Who are you that follow me with stealthy silent steps?

Ah, I know, it is your desire to rob me of all my gains. I will not disappoint you!

For I still have something left, and my fate has not cheated me of everything.

夜半到家。我两手空空。

你带着切望的眼睛，在门前等我，无眠而静默。

像一只羞怯的鸟，你满怀热爱地飞到我胸前。

哎，哎，我的神，我还有许多剩余。命运并没有把我的一切都骗走。

At midnight I reach home. My hands are empty.

You are waiting with anxious eyes at my door, sleepless and silent.

Like a timorous bird you fly to my breast with eager love.

Ay, ay, my God, much remains still. My fate has not cheated me of everything.

072

用了几天的苦工，我盖起一座庙宇。这庙里没有门窗，墙壁是用层石厚厚地垒起的。

我忘掉一切，我躲避大千世界，我神注目夺地凝视着我安放在龛里的偶像。

里面永远是黑夜，以香油的灯盏来照明。

不断的香烟，把我的心缭绕在沉重的螺旋里。

我彻夜不眠，用扭曲混乱的线条在墙上刻画出一些奇异的图形——生翼的马，人面的花，四肢像蛇的女人。

我不在任何地方留下一线之路，使鸟的歌声，叶的细语，或村镇的喧嚣得以进入。

在沉黑的仰顶上，唯一的声音是我礼赞的回响。

我的心思变得强烈而镇定，像一个尖尖的火焰。我的感官在狂欢中昏晕。

我不知时间如何度过，直到巨雷震劈了这座庙宇，一阵剧痛刺穿我的心。

With days of hard travail I raised a temple. It had no doors or windows, its walls were thickly built with massive stones.

I forgot all else. I shunned all the world, I gazed in rapt contemplation at the image I had set upon the altar.

It was always night inside, and lit by the lamps of perfumed oil.

The ceaseless smoke of incense wound my heart in its heavy coils.

Sleepless, I carved on the walls fantastic figures in mazy bewildering lines—winged horses, flowers with human faces, women with limbs like serpents.

No passage was left anywhere through which could enter the song of birds, the murmur of leaves, or hum of the busy village.

The only sound that echoed in its dark dome was that of incantations which I chanted.

My mind became keen and still like a pointed flame, my senses swooned in ecstasy.

I knew not how time passed till the thunder-stone had struck the temple, and a pain stung me through the heart.

灯火显得苍白而羞愧；墙上的刻画像是被锁住的梦，无意义地瞪视着，仿佛要躲藏起来。

我看着龛上的偶像。我看见它微笑了，和神的活生生的接触，它活了起来。被我囚禁的黑夜，展起翅来飞逝了。

The lamp looked pale and ashamed; the carvings on the walls, like chained dreams, stared meaningless in the light as they would fain hide themselves.

I looked at the image on the altar. I saw it smiling and alive with the living touch of God. The night I had imprisoned had spread its wings and vanished.

073

无量的财富不是你的，我的耐心的微黑的尘土母亲。

你操劳着来填满你孩子们的嘴，但是粮食是很少的。

你给我们的欢乐礼物，永远不是完全的。

你给你孩子们做的玩具，是不牢的。

你不能满足我们的一切渴望，但是我能为此就背弃你么？

你的含着痛苦阴影的微笑，对我的眼睛是甜柔的。

你的永不满足的爱，对我的心是亲切的。

从你的胸乳里，你是以生命而不是以不朽来哺育我们，因此你的眼睛永远是警醒的。

累年积代地你用颜色和诗歌来工作，但是你的天堂还没有盖起，仅有天堂的愁苦的意味。

你的美的创造上蒙着泪雾。

我将把我的诗歌倾注入你无言的心里，把我的爱倾注入你的爱中。

我将用劳动来礼拜你。

我看见过你的温慈的面庞，我爱你的悲哀的尘土，大地母亲。

Infinite wealth is not yours, my patient and dusky mother dust!

You toil to fill the mouths of your children, but food is scarce.

The gift of gladness that you have for us is never perfect.

The toys that you make for your children are fragile.

You cannot satisfy all our hungry hopes, but should I desert you for that?

Your smile which is shadowed with pain is sweet to my eyes.

Your love which knows not fulfillment is dear to my heart.

From your breast you have fed us with life but not immortality, that is why your eyes are ever wakeful.

For ages you are working with colour and song, yet your heaven is not built, but only its sad suggestion.

Over your creations of beauty there is the mist of tears.

I will pour my songs into your mute heart, and my love into your love.

I will worship you with labour.

I have seen your tender face and I love your mournful dust, Mother Earth.

074

在世界的谒见堂里，一根朴素的草叶，和阳光与夜半的星辰，坐在同一条毡褥上。

我的诗歌，也这样地和云彩与森林的音乐，在世界的心中平分席次。

但是，你这富有的人，你的财富，在太阳的喜悦的金光和沉思的月亮的柔光这种单纯的光彩里，却占不了一份。

包罗万象的天空的祝福，没有洒在它的上面。

等到死亡出现的时候，它就苍白枯萎，碎成尘土了。

In the world's audience hall, the simple blade of grass sits on the same carpet with the sunbeam and the stars of midnight.

Thus my songs share their seats in the heart of the world with the music of the clouds and forests.

But, you man of riches, your wealth has no part in the simple grandeur of the sun's glad gold and the mellow gleam of the musing moon.

The blessing of all-embracing sky is not shed upon it.

And when death appears, it pales and withers and crumbles into dust.

075

夜半，那个自称的苦行人宣告说：

"弃家求神的时候到了。呵，谁把我牵住在妄想里这么久呢？"

神低声说："是我。"但是这个人的耳朵是塞住的。

他的妻子和吃奶的孩子一同躺着，安静地睡在床的那边。

这个人说："什么人把我骗了这么久呢？"

声音又说："是神。"但是他听不见。

婴儿在梦中哭了，挨向他的母亲。

神命令说："别走，傻子，不要离开你的家。"但是他还是听不见。

神叹息又委屈地说："为什么我的仆人要把我丢下，而到处去找我呢？"

At midnight the would-be ascetic announced:

"This is the time to give up my home and seek for God. Ah, who has held me so long in delusion here?"

God whispered, "I," but the ears of the man were stopped.

With a baby asleep at her breast lay his wife, peacefully sleeping on one side of the bed.

The man said, "Who are ye that have fooled me so long?"

The voice said again, "They are God," but he heard it not.

The baby cried out in its dream, nestling close to its mother.

God commanded, "Stop, fool, leave not thy home," but still he heard not.

God sighed and complained, "Why does my servant wander to seek me, forsaking me?"

076

庙前的集会正在进行。从一早起就下雨，这一天快过尽了。

比一切群众的欢乐还光辉的，是一个花一文钱买到一个棕叶哨子的小女孩的光辉的微笑。

哨子的尖脆欢乐的声音，在一切笑语喧哗之上飘浮。

无尽的人流挤在一起，路上泥泞，河水在涨，雨在不停地下着，田地都没在水里。

比一切群众的烦恼更深的，是一个小男孩的烦恼——他连买那根带颜色的小棍的一文钱都没有。

他苦闷的眼睛望着那间小店，使得这整个人类的集会变成可悲悯的。

The fair was on before the temple. It had rained from the early morning and the day came to its end.

Brighter than all the gladness of the crowd was the bright smile of a girl who bought for a farthing a whistle of palm leaf.

The shrill joy of that whistle floated above all laughter and noise.

An endless throng of people came and jostled together.

The road was muddy, the river in flood, the field under water in ceaseless rain.

Greater than all the troubles of the crowd was a little boy's trouble—he had not a farthing to buy a painted stick.

His wistful eyes gazing at the shop made this whole meeting of men so pitiful.

077

西乡来的工人和他的妻子正忙着替砖窑挖土。

他们的小女儿到河边的渡头上；她无休无歇地擦洗锅盘。

她的小弟弟，光着头，赤裸着黳黑的涂满泥土的身躯，跟着她，听她的话，在高高的河岸上耐心地等着她。

她顶着满瓶的水，平稳地走回家去，左手提着发亮的铜壶，右手拉着那个孩子——她是妈妈的小丫头，繁重的家务使她变得严肃了。

有一天我看见那赤裸的孩子伸着腿坐着。

他姐姐坐在水里，用一把土在转来转去地擦洗一把水壶。

一只毛茸茸的小羊，在河岸上吃草。

它走近这孩子身边，忽然大叫了一声，孩子吓得哭喊起来。

他姐姐放下水壶跑上岸来。

她一只手抱起弟弟，一只手抱起小羊，把她的爱抚分成两半，人类和动物的后代在慈爱的连结中合一了。

The workman and his wife from the west country are busy digging to make bricks for the kiln.

Their little daughter goes to the landing-place by the

river; there she has no end of scouring and scrubbing of pots and pans.

Her little brother, with shaven head and brown, naked, mud-covered limbs, follows after her and waits patiently on the high bank at her bidding.

She goes back home with the full pitcher poised on her head, the shining brass pot in her left hand, holding the child with her right—she the tiny servant of her mother, grave with the weight of the household cares.

One day I saw this naked boy sitting with legs outstretched.

In the water his sister sat rubbing a drinking-pot with a handful of earth, turning it round and round.

Nearby a soft-haired lamb stood grazing along the bank.

It came close to where the boy sat and suddenly bleated aloud, and the child started up and screamed.

His sister left off cleaning her pot and ran up.

She took up her brother in one arm and the lamb in the other, and dividing her caresses between them bound in one bond of affection the offspring of beast and man.

078

在五月天里。闷热的正午仿佛无尽地悠长。干地在灼热中渴得张着口。

当我听到河边有个声音叫道："来吧，我的宝贝！"

我合上书开窗外视。

我看见一只皮毛上尽是泥土的大水牛，眼光沉着地站在河边；一个小伙子站在没膝的水里，在叫它来洗澡。

我高兴而微笑了，我心里感到一阵甜柔的接触。

It was in May. The sultry noon seemed endlessly long. The dry earth gaped with thirst in the heat.

When I heard from the riverside a voice calling, "Come, my darling!"

I shut my book and opened the window to look out.

I saw a big buffalo with mud-stained hide standing near the river with placid, patient eyes; and a youth, knee-deep in water, calling it to its bath.

I smiled amused and felt a touch of sweetness in my heart.

079

我常常思索，人和动物之间没有语言，他们心中互相认识的界线在哪里。

在远古创世的清晨，通过哪一条太初乐园的单纯的小径，他们的心曾彼此访问过。

他们的亲属关系早被忘却，他们不变的足印的符号并没有消灭。

可是忽然在那无言的音乐中，那模糊的记忆清醒起来，动物用温柔的信任注视着人的脸，人也用嬉嬉笑的感情下望着它的眼睛。

好像两个朋友戴着面具相逢，在伪装下彼此模糊地互认着。

I often wonder where lie hidden the boundaries of recognition between man and the beast whose heart knows no spoken language.

Through what primal paradise in a remote morning of creation ran the simple path by which their hearts visited each other?

Those marks of their constant tread have not been effaced

though their kinship has been long forgotten.

Yet suddenly in some wordless music the dim memory wakes up and the beast gazes into the man's face with a tender trust, and the man looks down into its eyes with amused affection.

It seems that the two friends meet masked and vaguely know each other through the disguise.

080

用一转的秋波，你能从诗人的琴弦上夺去一切诗歌的财富，美妙的女人！

但是你不愿听他们的赞扬，因此我来颂赞你。

你能使世界上最骄傲的头在你脚前俯伏。

但是你愿意崇拜的是你所爱的没有名望的人们，因此我崇拜你。

你的完美的双臂的接触，能在帝王的荣光上加上光荣。

但你却用你的手臂去扫除尘土，使你微贱的家庭整洁，因此我心中充满了钦敬。

With a glance of your eyes you could plunder all the wealth of songs struck from poets'harps, fair woman!

But for their praises you have no ear, therefore I come to praise you.

You could humble at your feet the proudest heads in the world.

But it is your loved ones, unknown to fame, whom you choose to worship, therefore I worship you.

The perfection of your arms would add glory to kingly splendour with their touch.

But you use them to sweep away the dust, and to make clean your humble home, therefore I am filled with awe.

081

你为什么这样低声地对我耳语，呵，"死亡"，我的"死亡"？

当花儿晚谢，牛儿归棚，你偷偷地走到我身边，说出我不了解的话语。

难道你必须用昏沉的微语和冰冷的接吻，来向我求爱来赢得我心么，呵，"死亡"，我的"死亡"？

Why do you whisper so faintly in my ears, O Death, my Death?

When the flowers droop in the evening and cattle come back to their stalls, you stealthily come to my side and speak words that I do not understand.

Is this how you must woo and win me, with the opiate of drowsy murmur and cold kisses, O Death, my Death?

我们的婚礼不会有铺张的仪式么？

在你褐黄的鬈发上不系上花串么?

在你前面没有举旗的人么? 你也没有通红的火炬, 使黑夜像着火一样地明亮么, 呵, "死亡", 我的 "死亡"?

Will there be no proud ceremony for our wedding?

Will you not tie up with a wreath your tawny coiled locks?

Is there none to cany your banner before you, and will not the night be on fire with your red torch-lights, O Death, my Death?

你吹着法螺来吧, 在无眠之夜来吧。

给我穿上红衣, 紧握我的手把我娶走吧。

让你的驾着急躁嘶叫的马的车辇, 准备好等在我门前吧。

揭开我的面纱骄傲地看我的脸吧, 呵, "死亡", 我的 "死亡"!

Come with your conch-shells sounding, come in the sleepless night.

Dress me with a crimson mantle, grasp my hand and take me.

Let your chariot be ready at my door with your horses neighing impatiently.

Raise my veil and look at my face proudly, O Death, my Death!

082

我们今夜要做"死亡"的游戏，我的新娘和我。

夜是深黑的，空中的云霾是翻腾的，波涛在海里咆哮。

我们离开梦的床榻，推门出去，我的新娘和我。

我们坐在秋千上，狂风从后面猛烈地推送我们。

我的新娘吓得又惊又喜，她颤抖着紧靠在我的胸前。

许多日子我温存地服侍她。

我替她铺一个花床，我关上门不让强烈的光射在她眼上。

我轻轻地吻她的嘴唇，软软地在她耳边低语，直到她困倦得半入昏睡。

她消失在模糊的无边甜柔的云雾之中。

我摩抚她，她没有反应；我的歌唱也不能把她唤醒。

今夜，风暴的召唤从旷野来到。

We are to play the game of death to-night, my bride and I.

The night is black, the clouds in the sky are capricious, and the waves are raving at sea.

We have left our bed of dreams, flung open the door and

come out, my bride and I.

We sit upon a swing, and the storm-winds give us a wild push from behind.

My bride starts up with fear and delight, she trembles and clings to my breast.

Long have I served her tenderly.

I made for her a bed of flowers and I closed the doors to shut out the rude light from her eyes.

I kissed her gently on her lips and whispered softly in her ears till she half swooned in languor.

She was lost in the endless mist of vague sweetness.

She answered not to my touch, my songs failed to arouse her.

To-night has come to us the call of the storm from the wild.

我的新娘颤抖着站起，她牵着我的手走了出来。

她的头发在风中飞扬，她的面纱飘动，她的花环在胸前习习作响。

死亡的推送把她摇晃活了。

我们面面相看，心心相印，我的新娘和我。

My bride has shivered and stood up, she has clasped my hand and come out.

Her hair is flying in the wind, her veil is fluttering, her garland rustles over her breast.

The push of death has swung her into life.

We are face to face and heart to heart, my bride and I.

083

她住在玉米地边的山畔，靠近那股嘻嘻笑着流经古树的庄严的阴影的清泉。女人们提罐到这里来装水，过客们在这里谈话休息。她每天随着潺潺的泉韵工作幻想。

有一天，一个陌生人从云中的山上下来；他的头发像醉蛇一样地纷乱。我们惊奇地问："你是谁？"他不回答，只坐在喧闹的水边沉默地望着她的茅屋。我们吓得心跳，到了夜里我们都回家去了。

第二天早晨，女人们到杉树下的泉边取水，她们发现她茅屋的门开着，但是，她的声音没有了，她的微笑的脸哪里去了呢？空罐立在地上，她屋角的灯，油尽火灭了。没有人晓得在黎明以前她跑到哪里去了——那个陌生人也不见了。

She dwelt on the hillside by the edge of a maize-field, near the spring that flows in laughing rills through the solemn shadows of ancient trees. The women came there to fill their jars, and travellers would sit there to rest and talk. She worked and dreamed daily to the tune of the bubbling stream.

One evening the stranger came down from the cloud-hidden peak; his locks were tangled like drowsy snakes. We asked in wonder, "Who are you?" He answered not but sat by the garrulous stream and silently gazed at the hut where she dwelt. Our hearts quaked in fear and we came back home when it was night.

Next morning when the women came to fetch water at the spring by the deodar trees, they found the doors open in her hut, but her voice was gone and where was her smiling face? The empty jar lay on the floor and her lamp had burnt itself out in the corner. No one knew where she had fled to before it was morning—and the stranger had gone.

到了五月，阳光渐强，冰雪化尽，我们坐在泉边哭泣。我们心里想："她去的地方有泉水么，在这炎热焦渴的天气中，她能到哪里去取水呢？"我们惶恐地对问："在我们住的山外还有地方么？"

夏天的夜里，微风从南方吹来；我坐在她的空屋里，没有点上的灯仍在那里立着。忽然间那座山峰，像帘幕拉开一样从我眼前消失了。"呵，那是她来了。你好么，我的孩子？你快乐么？在无遮的天空下，你有个荫凉的地方么？可怜呵，我们的泉水不在这里供你解渴。"

"那边还是那个天空，"她说，"只是不受屏山的遮隔，——也还是那股流泉长成江河，——也还是那片土地伸广变成平原。""一切都有了，"我叹息说，"只有我们不在。"她含愁地笑着说，"你们是在我的心里。"我醒起听见泉流潺潺，杉树的叶子在夜中沙沙地响着。

In the month of May the sun grew strong and the snow melted, and we sat by the spring and wept. We wondered in our mind, "Is there a spring in the land where she has gone and where she can fill her vessel in these hot thirsty days?" And we asked each other in dismay, "Is there a land beyond these hills where we live?"

It was a summer night; the breeze blew from the south; and I sat in her deserted room where the lamp stood still unlit. When suddenly from before my eyes the hills vanished like curtains drawn aside. "Ah, it is she who comes. How are you, my child? Are you happy? But where can you shelter under this open sky? And, alas, our spring is not here to allay your thirst."

"Here is the same sky," she said, "only free from the fencing hills, —this is the same stream grown into a river, — the same earth widened into a plain." "Everything is here," I sighed, "only we are not." She smiled sadly and said. "You are in my heart." I woke up and heard the babbling of the stream and the rustling of the deodars at night.

084

黄绿的稻田上掠过秋云的阴影，后面是狂追的太阳。

蜜蜂被光明所陶醉；忘了吸蜜，只痴呆地飞翔嗡唱。

河里岛上的鸭群，无缘无故地欢乐地吵闹。

我们都不回家吧，兄弟们，今天早晨我们都不去工作。

让我们以狂风暴雨之势占领青天，让我们飞奔着抢夺空间吧。

笑声飘浮在空气上，像洪水上的泡沫。

弟兄们，让我们把清晨浪费在无用的歌曲上面吧。

Over the green and yellow rice-fields sweep the shadows of the autumn clouds followed by the swift-chasing sun.

The bees forget to sip their honey; drunken with light they foolishly hover and hum.

The ducks in the islands of the river clamour in joy for mere nothing.

Let none go back home, brothers, this morning, let none go to work.

Let us take the blue sky by storm and plunder space as we run.

Laughter floats in the air like foam on the flood.

Brothers, let us squander our morning in futile songs.

085

你是什么人，读者，百年后读着我的诗？

我不能从春天的财富里送你一朵花，从天边的云彩里送你一片金影。

开起门来四望吧。

从你的群花盛开的园子里，采取百年前消逝了的花儿的芬芳记忆。

在你心的欢乐里，愿你感到一个春晨吟唱的活的欢乐，把它快乐的声音，传过一百年的时间。

Who are you, reader, reading my poems a hundred years hence?

I cannot send you one single flower from this wealth of the spring, one single streak of gold from yonder clouds.

Open your doors and look abroad.

From your blossoming garden gather fragrant memories of the vanished flowers of a hundred years before.

In the joy of your heart may you feel the living joy that sang one spring morning, sending its glad voice across a hundred years.

徐志摩 1924 年 5 月 12 日在北京真光剧场的演讲

我有几句话想趁这个机会对诸君讲，不知道你们有没有耐心听。泰戈尔先生快走了，在几天内他就离别北京，在一两个星期内他就告辞中国。他这一去大约是不会再来的了。也许他永远不能再到中国。

他是六七十岁的老人，他非但身体不强健，他并且是有病的。所以他要到中国来，不但他的家属，他的亲戚朋友，他的医生，都不愿意他冒险，就是他欧洲的朋友，比如法国的罗曼·罗兰，也都有信去劝阻他。他自己也曾经踌躇了好久，他心里常常盘算他如其到中国来，他究竟能不能够给我们好处，他想中国人自有他们的诗人、思想家、教育家，他们有他们的智慧、天才、心智的财富与营养，他们更用不着外来的补助与戟刺，我只是一个诗人，我没有宗教家的福音，没有哲学家的理论，更没有科学家实利的效用，或是工程师建设的才能，他们要我去做什么，我自己又为什么要去，我有什么礼物带去满足他们的盼望。他真的很觉得迟疑，所以他延迟了他的行期。但是他也对我们说到冬天完了春风吹动的时候（印度的春风比我们的吹得早），他不由的感觉了一种内迫的冲动，他面对着逐渐滋长的青草与鲜花，不由的抛弃了，忘却了他应尽的职务，不由的解放了他的歌唱的本能，和着新来的鸣雀，在柔软的南风中开怀的讴吟。同时他收到我们催请的信，我们青年盼望他的诚意与热心，唤起了老人的勇气。他立即定夺了他东来的决心。他说趁我暮年的肢体不曾僵透，趁我衰老的心灵还能感受，决不可错过这最后唯一的机会，这博大、从容、礼让的民族，我幼年时便发心朝拜，与其将来在黄昏寂静的境界中萎衰的惆怅，毋宁利用这夕阳未暝的光芒，了却我晋香人的心愿？

他所以决意的东来，他不顾亲友的劝阻，医生的警告，不顾自身的高年与病体，他也撇开了在本国一切的任务，跋涉了万里的海程，他来到了中国。

自从四月十二在上海登岸以来，可怜老人不曾有过一半天完整的休息，旅行的劳顿不必说，单就公开的演讲以及较小集会时的谈话，至少也有了三四十次！他的，我们知道，不是教授们的讲义，不是教士们的讲道，他的心府不是堆积货品的栈房，他的辞令不是教科书的喇叭。他是灵活的泉水，一颗颗颤动的圆珠从他心里兢兢的泛登水面都是生命的精液；他是瀑布的吼声，在白云间，青林中，石罅里，不住的欢响；他是百灵的歌声，他的欢欣、愤慨、响亮的谐音，弥漫在无际的晴空。但是他是倦了。终夜的狂歌已经耗尽了子规的精力，东方的曙色亦照出他点点的心血染红了蔷薇枝上的白露。

老人是疲乏了。这几天他睡眠也不得安宁，他已经透支了他有限的精力。他差不多是靠散拿吐瑾①过日的。他不由的不感觉风尘的厌倦，他时常想念他少年时在恒河边沿拍浮的清福，他想望椰树的清荫与曼果的甜瓤。

但他还不仅是身体的惫劳，他也感觉心境的不舒畅。这是很不幸的。我们做主人的只是深深的负歉。他这次来华，不为游历，不为政治，更不为私人的利益，他熬着高年，冒着病体，抛弃自身的事业，备尝行旅的辛苦，他究竟为的是什么？他为的只是一点看不见的情感，说远一点，他的使命是在修补中国与印度两民族间中断千余年的桥梁。说近一点，他只想感召我们青年真挚的同情。因为他是信仰生命的，他是尊崇青年的，他是歌颂青春与清晨的，他永远指点着前途的光明。悲悯是当初释迦牟尼证果的动机，悲悯也是泰戈尔先生不辞艰苦的动机。现代的文明只是骇人的浪费，贪淫与残暴，自私与自大，相猜与相忌，飓风似的倾覆了人道的平衡，产生了巨大的毁灭。芜秽的心田里只是误解的蔓草，毒害同情的种子，更没有收成的希冀。在这个荒惨的境地里，难得有少数的丈夫，不怕阻难，不自馁怯，肩上扛着铲除误解的大锄，口袋里满装着新鲜人道的种子，不问天时是阴是雨是晴，不问是早晨是黄昏是黑夜，他只是努力的工作，清理一方泥土，施殖一方生命，同时口唱着嘹亮的新歌，鼓舞在黑暗中将次透露的萌芽。泰戈尔先生就是这少数中的一个。他是来广布同情的，他是来消除成见的。我们亲眼见过他慈祥的阳春似的表情，亲耳听过他从心灵底里迸裂出的大声，我想只要我们的良心不曾受恶毒的烟煤

---

① 散拿吐瑾：一种药物。

熏黑，或是被恶浊的偏见污抹，谁不曾感觉他至诚的力量，魔术似的，为我们生命的前途开辟了一个神奇的境界，燃点了理想的光明？所以我们也懂得他的深刻的懊怅与失望，如其他知道部分的青年不但不能容纳他的灵感，并且存心的诬毁他的热忱。我们固然奖励思想的独立，但我们决不敢附和误解自由。他生平最满意的成绩就在他永远能得青年的同情，不论在德国，在丹麦，在美国，在日本，青年永远是他最忠心的朋友。他也曾经遭受种种的误解与攻击，政府的猜疑与报纸的诬捏与守旧派的讥评，不论如何的谬妄与剧烈，从不曾扰动他优容的大量，他的希望，他的信仰，他的爱心，他的至诚，完全的托付青年。我的须，我的发是白的，但我的心却永远是青的，他常常的对我们说，只要青年是我的知己，我理想的将来就有着落，我乐观的明灯永远不致黯淡。他不能相信纯洁的青年也会坠落在怀疑、猜忌、卑琐的泥溷，他更不能信中国的青年也会沾染不幸的污点。他真不预备在中国遭受意外的待遇。他很不自在，他很感觉异样的怆心。

因此精神的懊丧更加重他躯体的倦劳。他差不多是病了。我们当然很焦急的期望他的健康，但他再没有心境继续他的讲演。我们恐怕今天就是他在北京公开讲演最后的一个机会。他有休养的必要。我们也决不忍再使他耗费有限的精力。他不久又有长途的跋涉，他不能不有三四天完全的养息。所以从今天起，所有已经约定的集会，公开与私人的，一概撤销，他今天就出城去静养。

我们关切他的一定可以原谅，就是一小部分不愿意他来作客的诸君也可以自喜战略的成功。他是病了，他在北京不再开口了，他快走了，他从此不再来了。但是同学们，我们也得平心的想想，老人到底有什么罪，他有什么负心，他有什么不可容赦的犯案？公道是死了么？为什么听不见你的声音？

他们说他是守旧，说他是顽固。我们能相信吗？他们说他是"太迟"，说他是"不合时宜"，我们能相信吗？他自己是不能信，真的不能信。他说这一定是滑稽家的反调。他一生所遭逢的批评只是太新，太早，太急进，太激烈，太革命的，太理想的，他六十年的生涯只是不断的奋斗与冲锋，他现在还只是冲锋与奋斗。但是他们说他是守旧，太迟，太老。他顽固奋斗的对象只是暴烈主义、资本主义、帝国主义、武力主义、杀灭性灵的物质主义；他主张的只是创造的生活，心灵的自由，国际的和平，教育的改造，普爱的实现。但他们说他是帝国政策的间谍，资本主义的助力，亡国奴族的流民，提倡裹脚的狂人！肮脏是在我们的政客与暴徒的心里，与我们的诗人又有什么关系？昏乱是在我们冒名的学者与文人的脑里，与我们的诗人又有什么亲属？我们何妨说太阳是黑的，我们何妨说苍蝇是真理？同学们，听信我的话，像他的这样伟大的声音我们也许一辈子再不会听着的了。留神目前的机会，预防将来的惆怅！他的人格我们只能到历史上去搜寻比拟。他的博大的温柔的灵魂我敢说永远是人类记忆里的一次灵绩。他的无边的想象与辽阔的同情使我们想起惠德曼①；他的博爱的福音与宣传的热心使我们记起托尔斯泰；他的坚韧的意志与艺术的天才使我们

---

① 惠德曼：通译为惠特曼（1819—1892），美国诗人，著有《草叶集》等。

想起造摩西①像的密仡郎其罗②；他的诙谐与智慧使我们想象当年的苏格拉底与老聃！他的人格的和谐与优美使我们想念暮年的葛德；他的慈祥的纯爱的抚摩，他的为人道不厌的努力，他的磅礴的大声，有时竟使我们唤起救主的心像，他的光彩，他的音乐，他的雄伟，使我们想念奥林必克③山顶的大神。他是不可侵凌的，不可逾越的，他是自然界的一个神秘的现象。他是三春和暖的南风，惊醒树枝上的新芽，增添处女颊上的红晕。他是普照的阳光。他是一派浩瀚的大水，来从不可追寻的渊源，在大地的怀抱中终古的流着，不息的流着，我们只是两岸的居民，凭借这慈恩的天赋，灌溉我们的田稻，苏解我们的消渴，洗净我们的污垢。他是喜马拉雅积雪的山峰，一般的崇高，一般的纯洁，一般的壮丽，一般的高傲，只有无限的青天枕藉他银白的头颅。

　　人格是一个不可错误的实在，荒歉是一件大事，但我们是饿惯了的，只认鸠形与鹄面是人生本来的面目，永远忘却了真健康的颜色与彩泽。标准的低降是一种可耻的堕落：我们只是踞坐在井底青蛙，但我们更没有怀疑的余地。我们也许揣详东方的初白，却不能非议中天的太阳。我们也许见惯了阴霾的天时，不耐这热烈的光焰，消散天空的云雾，暴露地面的荒芜，但同时在我们心灵的深处，我们岂不也感觉一个新鲜的影响，催促我们生命的跳动，

---

① 摩西：《圣经》故事中古代犹太人的领袖。

② 密仡郎其罗：通译为米开朗基罗（1475—1564），意大利文艺复兴时期的雕塑家、画家。

③ 奥林必克：通译为奥林匹斯，希腊东北部的一座高山，古代希腊人视为神山，希腊神话中的诸神都住在山顶。

唤醒潜在的想望，仿佛是武士望见了前峰烽烟的信号，更不踌躇的奋勇前向？只有接近了这样超轶的纯粹的丈夫，这样不可错误的实在，我们方始相形的自愧我们的口不够阔大，我们的嗓音不够响亮，我们的呼吸不够深长，我们的信仰不够坚定，我们的理想不够莹澈，我们的自由不够磅礴，我们的语言不够明白，我们的情感不够热烈，我们的努力不够勇猛，我们的资本不够充实……

我自信我不是恣滥不切事理的崇拜，我如其曾经应用浓烈的文字，这是因为我不能自制我浓烈的感想。但是我最急切要声明的是，我们的诗人，虽则常常招受神秘的徽号，在事实上却是最清明，最有趣，最诙谐，最不神秘的生灵。他是最通达人情，最近人情的。我盼望有机会追写他日常的生活与谈话。如其我是犯嫌疑的，如其我也是性近神秘的（有好多朋友这么说），你们还有适之^①先生的见证，他也说他是最可爱最可亲的个人：我们可以相信适之先生绝对没有"性近神秘"的嫌疑！所以无论他怎样的伟大与深厚，我们的诗人还只是有骨有血的人，不是野人，也不是天神。唯其是人，尤其是最富情感的人，所以他到处要求人道的温暖与安慰，他尤其要我们中国青年的同情与情爱。他已经为我们尽了责任，我们不应，更不忍辜负他的期望。同学们！爱你的爱，崇拜你的崇拜，是人情不是罪孽，是勇敢不是懦怯！

---

① 适之：胡适（1891—1962），当时是北京大学教授。

泰戈尔来华 [1]（徐志摩）

  泰戈尔在中国，不仅已得普遍的知名，竟是受普遍的景仰。问他爱念谁的英文诗，十余岁的小学生，就自信不疑地答说泰戈尔。在新诗界中，除了几位最有名的神形毕肖的泰戈尔的私淑弟子以外，十首作品里至少有八九首是受他直接或间接的影响的。这是可惊的状况，一个外国的诗人，能有这样普及的引力。

  现在他快到中国来了，在他青年的崇拜者听了，不消说，当然是最可喜的消息，他们不仅天天竖耳企踵地在盼望，就是他们梦里的颜色，我猜想，也一定多增了几分妩媚。现世界是个堕落沉寂的世界；我们往常要求一二伟大圣洁的人格给我们精神的慰安时，每每不得已上溯已往的历史，与神化的学士艺才，结想象

---

[1] 泰戈尔来华：泰戈尔来中国访问。这次讲学是由梁启超、蔡元培等人主持的讲学社出面邀请的，初拟1923年秋天成行，后因诗人身体原因延至第二年4月。他在中国期间，访问过上海、杭州、南京、武昌、济南、北京等地，做过多次讲演。徐志摩是这次活动的主持人兼翻译。这篇文章刊登于1923年的《小说月报》。

的因缘，哲士、诗人与艺术家，代表一民族一时代特具的天才；可怜华族，千年来只在精神穷窭中度活，真生命只是个追忆不全的梦境，真人格亦只似昏夜池水里的花草映影，在有无虚实之间，谁不想念春秋战国才智之盛；谁不咏慕屈子之悲歌，司马之大声，李白之仙音；谁不长念庄生之逍遥，东坡之风流，渊明之冲淡？我每想及过去的光荣，不禁疑问现时人荒心死的现象，莫非是噩梦的虚景，否则何以我们民族的灵海中，曾经有过偌大的潮迹，如今何至于沉寂如此？孔陵前子贡手植的楷树，圣庙中孔子手植的桧树，如其传话是可信的，过了二千几百年，经了几度的灾劫，到现在还不时有新枝从旧根上生发；我们华族天才的活力，难道还不如此桧此楷？

什么是自由？自由是不绝的心灵活动之表现。斯拉夫民族自开国起直至十九世纪中期，只是个庞大喑哑的无光的空气中苟活的怪物，但近六七十年来天才累出，突发大声，不但惊醒了自身，并且惊醒了所有迷梦的邻居。斯拉夫伟奥可怖的灵魂之发现，是百年来人类史上最伟大的一件事迹。华族往往以睡狮自比，这又泄漏我们想象力之堕落；期望一民族回复或取得吃人噬兽的暴力者，只是最下流"富国强兵教"的信徒，我们希望以后文化的意义与人类的目的明定以后，这类的谬见可以渐渐地销匿。

精神的自由，决不有待于政治或经济或社会制度之妥协，我们且看印度。印度不是我们所谓已亡之国么？我们常以印度、朝鲜、波兰并称，以为亡国的前例。我敢说我们见了印度人，不是发心怜悯，是意存鄙蔑（我想印度是最受一班人误解的民族，虽同在亚洲，大部分人以为印度人与马路上的红头阿三是一样同样的东西！）就政治看来，说我们比他们比较地有自由，这话勉强还可以说。但要论精神的自由，我们只似从前的俄国，是个庞大暗哑在无光的气圈中苟活的怪物，他们（印度）却有心灵活动的成绩，证明他们表面政治的奴缚非但不曾压倒，而且激动了他们潜伏的天才。在这时期他们连出了一个宗教性质的政治领袖——甘地——一个实行的托尔斯泰；两个大诗人，伽利达撒[①]（Kalidasa）与泰戈尔。单是甘地与泰戈尔的名字，就是印度民族不死的铁证。

东方人能以人格与作为，取得普通的崇拜与荣名者，不出在"国富兵强"的日本，不出在政权独立的中国，而出于亡国民族之印度——这不是应发人猛省的事实么？

泰戈尔在世界文学中，究占如何位置，我们此时还不能定，他的诗是否可算独立的贡献，他的思想是否可以代表印族复兴之潜流，他的哲学（如其他的哲学）是否有独到的境界——这些问题，我们没有回答的能力。但有一事我们敢断言肯定的。就是他不朽的人格。他的诗歌，他的思想，他的一切，都有遭遗忘与失时之可能，但他一生热奋的生涯所养成的人格，却是我们不易磨翳的纪念。〔泰戈尔生平的经过，我总觉得非是东方的，也许印度原不能算东方（陈寅恪[②]君在海外常常大放厥词，辩印度之为非

---

① 伽利达撒：通译为迦梨陀婆，印度古代诗人、剧作家，生于公元3—5世纪的笈多王朝。代表作有《沙恭达罗》等。

② 陈寅恪（1890—1969）：历史学家，早年留学日本、德国研究梵文。归国后，任清华大学教授。

东方的。)] 所以他这回来华，我个人最大的盼望，不在他更推广他诗艺的影响，不在传说他宗教的哲学的乃至于玄学的思想，而在他可爱的人格，给我们见得到他的青年，一个伟大深入的神感。他一生所走的路，正是我们现代努力于文艺的青年不可免的方向。他一生只是个不断的热烈的努力，向内开豁他天赋的才智，自然吸收应有的营养。

他境遇虽则一流顺利，但物质生活的平易，并不反射他精神生活之不艰险。我们知道诗人、艺术家的生活，集中在外人捉摸不到的内心境界。历史上也许有大名人一生不受物质的苦难，但绝没有不经心灵界的狂风暴雨与沉郁黑暗时期者。葛德[①]是一生不愁衣食的显例，但他在七十六岁那年对他的友人说他一生不曾有过四星期的幸福，一生只是在烦恼痛苦劳力中。泰戈尔是东方的一个显例，他的伤痕也都在奥秘的灵府中的。

我们所以加倍地欢迎泰戈尔来华，因为他那高超和谐的人格，可以给我们不可计量的慰安，可以开发我们原来淤塞的心灵泉源，可以指示我们努力的方向与标准，可以纠正现代狂放恣纵的反常行为，可以摩挲我们想见古人的忧心，可以消平我们过渡时期张皇的意义，可以使我们扩大同情与爱心，可以引导我们入完全的梦境。

如其一时期的问题，可以综合成一个现代的问题，就只是"怎样做一个人？"泰戈尔在与我们所处相仿的境地中，已经很高尚地解决了他个人的问题，所以他是我们的导师、榜样。

----

① 葛德：通译为歌德，德国诗人。

他是个诗人，尤其是一个男子，一个纯粹的人，他最伟大的作品就是他的人格。这话是极普通的话，我所以要在此重复地说，为的是怕误解。人不怕受人崇拜，但最怕受误解的崇拜。葛德说，最使人难受的是无意识的崇拜。泰戈尔自己也常说及。他最初最后只是个诗人——艺术家如其你愿意——他即使有宗教的或哲理的思想，也只是他诗心偶然的流露，决不为哲学家谈哲学，或为宗教而训宗教的。有人喜欢拿他的思想比这个那个西洋的哲学，以为他是表现东方一部的时代精神与西方合流的；或是研究他究竟有几分的耶稣教几分是印度教——这类的比较学也许在性质偏爱的人觉得有意思，但于泰戈尔之为泰戈尔，是绝对无所发明的。譬如有人见了他在山氏尼开顿 ①（Santiniketan）学校里所用的晨祷：

Thou art our Father. Do you help us to know thee as Father. We bow down to Thee. Do thou never afflict us, O Father, by causing a separation between Thee and us. O thou self-revealing one, O Thou Parent of the universe, purge away the multitude of our sins, and send unto us whatever is good and noble. To Thee, from whom spring joy and goodness nay, who art all goodness

① 山氏尼开顿：通译为桑地尼克丹（又译为圣蒂尼克坦），印度北部的一个地方。泰戈尔于 1901 年在此创办桑地尼克丹学校，至 1921 年发展成国际大学。

thyself, to Thee we bow down now and for ever[1].

耶教人见了这段祷告一定拉本家，说泰戈尔准是皈依基督的，但回头又听见他们的晚祷：

The Deity who is in fire and water, nay, who pervades the Universe through and through and makes His abode in tiny plants and towering forests—to such a Deity we bow down for ever and ever[2].

这不是最明显的泛神论么？这里也许有 Lucretius[3]，也许有 Spinoza[4]，也许有 Upanishads[5]，但决不是天父云云的一神教，谁都看得出来。回头在揭檀迦利[6] 的诗里，又发现什么 Lia 既不是耶教的，又不是泛神论。结果把一般专好拿封条拿题签来支配一切的，绝对的糊涂住了，他们一看这事不易办，就说泰戈尔是诗人，不

---

① 这段英文的大意是："您是我们的上帝。您使我们明白何为上帝。我们向您膜拜。噢，上帝，您从不与我们分离，使我们免遭痛苦。您，启示之神，您宇宙万物之父，净化了我们诸多的罪孽。您赐给了我们仁慈和荣耀。有了您春天会欢笑，善良也会欣喜。您就是一切善的化身。我们永远向您膜拜。"

② 这段英文的大意是："上帝存在于水中，存在于火中，而且遍及宇宙万物。他居住在不起眼的草丛里，居住在树木参天的森林里——我们永远向这样的上帝膜拜。"

③ Lucretius：通译为卢克莱修（公元前 99—前 55），古罗马哲学家。

④ Spinoza：通译为斯宾诺莎（1632—1677），荷兰哲学家。

⑤ Upanishads：《奥义书》，印度《吠陀》圣典的最后部分。

⑥ 揭檀迦利：通译为《吉檀迦利》，泰戈尔的散文诗集。

是宗教家。也不是专门的哲学家。管他神是一个或是两个或是无数或是没有，诗人的标准，只是诗的境界之真；在一般人看来是不相容纳的冲突（因为他们只见字面），他看来只是一体的谐合（因为他能超文字而悟实在）。

同样的在哲理方面，也就有人分别研究，说他的人格论是近于讹的，说他的艺术论是受讹影响的……这也是劳而无功的。

自从有了大学教授以来，尤其是美国的教授，学生忙的是：比较哲学，比较宪法学，比较人种学，比较宗教学，比较教育学，比较这样，比较那样，结果他们意想把最高粹的思想艺术，也用比较的方法来研究——我看倒不如来一门比较大学教授学还有趣些!

思想之不是糟粕，艺术之不是凡品，就在他们本身有完全、独立、纯粹不可分析的性质。类不同便没有可比较性，拿西洋现成的宗教哲学的派别去比凑一个创造的艺术家，犹之拿唐采芝或王玉峰去比附真纯创造的音乐家一样的可笑，一样的隔着靴子搔痒。

我们只要能够体会泰戈尔诗化的人格，与领略他充满人格的诗文，已经尽够的了，此外的事自有专门的书呆子去顾管，不劳我们费心。

我乘便又想起一件事，一九一三年泰戈尔被选得诺贝尔奖金的电报到印度时，印度人听了立即发疯一般的狂喜，满街上小孩大人一齐呼庆祝，但诗人在家里，非但不乐，而且叹道："我从此没有安闲日子过了!"接着下年英政府又封他为爵士，从此，真的，他不曾有过安闲时日。他的山氏尼开顿竟变了朝拜的中心，他出游欧美时，到处受无上的欢迎，瑞典、丹麦几处学生，好像都为他举行火把会与提灯会，在德国听他讲演的往往累万，美国招待他的盛况，恐怕不在英国皇太子之下。但这是诗人所心愿的幸福么？固然我不敢说诗人便能完全免除虚荣心，但这类群众的哄动，大部分只是葛德所谓无意识的崇拜，真诗人决不会艳羡的，最可厌是西洋一般社交太太们，她们的宗教照例是英雄崇拜；英雄愈新奇，她们愈乐意，泰戈尔那样的道貌岸然，宽袍布帽，当然加倍地搔痒了她们的好奇心，大家要来和这远东的诗圣，握握手，亲热亲热，说几句照例的肉麻话……这是近代享盛名的一点小报应，我想性爱恬淡的泰戈尔先生，临到这种情形，真也是说不出的苦。据他的英友恩厚之告诉我们说他近来愈发厌烦嘈杂了，又且他身体也不十分能耐劳，但他就使不愿意，却也很少显示于外，所以他这次来华，虽则不至受社交太太们之窘，但我们有机会瞻仰他言论丰采的人，应该格外的体谅他，谈论时不过分去劳乏他，演讲能节省处节省，使他和我们能如家人一般地相与，能如在家乡一般地舒服，那才对得住他高年跋涉的一番至意。

七月六日

（原刊 1923 年 9 月 10 日《小说月报》第 14 卷第 9 号）